]

Garden Girls
Cozy Mystery Series Book 18

Hope Callaghan

***

hopecallaghan.com
Copyright © 2017
All rights reserved.

Visit my website for new releases and special offers: hopecallaghan.com

Thank you, Peggy H., Cindi G., Jean P., Barbara W. and Wanda D. for taking the time to preview *Dash for Cash,* for the extra sets of eyes and for catching all of my mistakes.

A special thanks to my reader review team: Alice, Amary, Barbara, Becky, Becky B, Brinda, Cassie, Christina, Debbie, Dee, Denota, Devan, Grace, Jan, Jo-Ann, Joeline, Joyce, Jean K., Jean M., Lynne, Megan, Melda, Kat, Linda, Lynne, Pat, Patsy, Paula, Rebecca, Renate, Rita, Rita P, Shelba, Tamara, Valerie and Vicki.

i

CONTENTS

Like Free eBooks?

Get Free & Discounted eBooks, Giveaways & New Releases When You Subscribe To My Free Cozy Mysteries Newsletter!

hopecallaghan.com/newsletter

Cast of Characters

Gloria Rutherford-Kennedy. Recently remarried, Gloria is the ringleader of her merry band of friends. She lives on a farm on the outskirts of Belhaven, a small town in West Michigan.

Lucy Carlson. Gloria's best friend. A bit of a weapon's expert and part-tomboy, Lucy enjoys shooting guns, riding four-wheelers and hunting...when she's not being dragged into one of Gloria's mysteries.

Dorothy Jenkins. Dorothy "Dot" Jenkins and her husband, Ray, are co-owners of Dot's Restaurant. The cautious one of the bunch, Dot would much rather stay on the sidelines during Gloria's adventures but most of the time it doesn't work out that way.

Margaret Hansen. Recently widowed, Margaret is learning to adjust to life alone. The most critical of the group of friends, Margaret tends to see everything in black and white with a tad of jaded.

Ruth Carpenter. Head postmaster of the Belhaven Post Office, Ruth is the queen of surveillance and is always up on the latest spy equipment. With her recently tricked out / customized, bulletproof van along with her high tech spy gear, Ruth is Gloria's right hand gal in many of her investigations.

Andrea Malone. The youngest member of the Garden Girls group, Andrea met Gloria and the others through a string of tragic events. Despite the fact that Gloria is protective of her young friend, Andrea is usually in the thick of all of Gloria's investigations.

"But godliness with contentment is great gain. For we brought nothing into the world, and we can take nothing out of it. But if we have food and clothing, we will be content with that." 1 Timothy 6: 6-8 NIV

Chapter 1

Gloria Rutherford-Kennedy peeked around the side of the towering stack of postcards. "Ruth...are you back there?"

Ruth, the Town of Belhaven's postmaster, turned to the side. "Hey Gloria. I thought I heard someone call my name." She pressed the postcards against her chest, keeping a tight grip with both hands as she carried them to the bin behind her.

Kenny Webber, Belhaven's rural route postal carrier, lifted an eyebrow and stared at the postcards. "You're mailing another batch of postcards? I hope you're not wasting your time."

"I'm not wasting my time. I figure this way the officials will know I'm serious about the contest." Ruth nudged the bin with her foot and hurried to the counter. "You're out early this morning."

"Paul started his security job at the new Rockville outdoor mall." Gloria shrugged her purse off her shoulder and set it on the counter. "It's going to take some time getting used to these early hours, but he seemed excited when he left." She nodded toward the bin. "What's this about a contest?"

"It's just a little project I'm working on."

Gloria's interest was piqued. "What sort of little project?"

Kenny snorted and Ruth shot him a death look. "A fmmble tnst."

"What?"

"I'm trying to snag a final spot in the new game show, Dash for Cash."

"Dash for Cash?" Gloria chuckled. "Isn't that the show where you have to jump through hoops, literally, to stay in the game?" Paul and she had watched the show several times, marveling at the crazy antics of both the show's host, Bob Larker, and the contestants who participated for chances to win cash and prizes.

"Are you saying I'm not up to it?" Ruth frowned.

"I..." Gloria paused. "You're serious."

"You bet I am. The show's producers are coming to Grand Rapids for the next round of eliminations." Ruth explained she'd already completed the test questions after weeks of submitting applications. "I figured I could increase my odds if I applied in person, too. You know, so they know I'm serious."

3

"Oh, she's serious all right," Kenny chimed in. "I've been putting her through the paces and she's mastered the endurance training. We're still working on the strength training."

Gloria's gaze fell to Kenny's midsection. "You're Ruth's trainer?"

Kenny patted his paunch. "I may have a few years on me and am a little out of shape, but a military man never forgets boot camp. I'll have Ruth in tiptop shape before the first round of eliminations." He waved at Ruth. "Show Gloria your guns."

Ruth tightened her jaw and stubbornly shook her head. "No."

Gloria pressed her hand to her mouth to hide a laugh. "C'mon Ruth. Show me your guns."

"All right." Ruth lifted her sleeve and flexed her muscles.

"Very impressive," Gloria said. "When exactly is the competition?"

"Next week." Ruth lowered her sleeve. "I joined an online chat group with some of the other contestants. I'm confident I have a shot at making it on the show."

"Except for the bodybuilder chick and the GI Joe trainer guy," Kenny said.

Ruth waved her hand dismissively. "The bigger they are, the harder they fall. Besides, they're just a bunch of braggarts. I doubt they've even been training. Plus, they're not going to have the secret weapon that I'm gonna have."

"Secret weapon?"

"Rose's special elixir. It's similar to the stuff she sells to Eleanor and her group, but more powerful. She says she's working on a batch guaranteed to make me stronger than the Incredible Hulk and more agile than Wonder Woman."

"Hopefully she doesn't turn you green," Gloria joked.

"I'm dead serious about this," Ruth said. "I've done my homework, and the cash and prizes are the best out there in game show land."

"Then I'm 100% behind you," Gloria said. "Let me know if there's anything I can do to help."

"Thanks Gloria. This is the most exciting thing that's happened since...well, since you found Vanessa Hines' body a few weeks ago."

"Yeah, things have been a little quiet around here, almost too quiet." Gloria mailed her package, exited the post office and crossed the street, making her way to Dot's Restaurant. The place was packed and even busier than normal.

Gloria suspected part of the reason was the opening of the new subdivision, Belhaven Corners. Business was booming and Dot and her husband, Ray, had placed an offer on the building next door to the restaurant, with tentative plans to expand.

She caught a glimpse of Dot in the back and gave a quick wave before easing into an empty seat in the corner.

Dot darted to the table. "You're out early." She reached for an empty coffee cup and began filling it.

"Yeah. Paul started his new job at Rockville's outdoor shopping mall, so we had to get up early."

"I haven't been there yet. I heard it's nice. Are you hungry?" Dot straightened.

"Nope. I ate with Paul." Gloria sipped her coffee and eyed her friend over the rim, noting the dark circles under Dot's eyes. "Are you feeling okay?"

"I-I'm a little tired. I haven't been sleeping well lately. I've had a lot on my mind the past few days." Dot glanced around and then slid into the empty seat across from Gloria. "I had my follow-up mammogram last week and the technician saw something, so they did a biopsy."

The blood drained from Gloria's face. "Do they suspect cancer again?"

"I don't know." Dot lowered her voice. "I haven't told anyone else. You're the first person, other than Ray. I didn't dare tell Rose since she would be mixing potions left and right."

"When will you find out?"

Dot shrugged. "It all depends on the lab. Last time, it took over a week to hear back." She stood. "At least this place keeps my mind off of it."

"I'm sorry to hear that, Dot. When you got your first diagnosis, you and Ray talked about slowing down, taking it easy. Are you sure you want to buy the building next door?"

"I'm not sure about anything," Dot admitted. "Ray and I have agreed to hold off on purchasing the building until we find out the test results. Please keep this under your hat. I don't want the others to know yet."

"Absolutely," Gloria said.

"Dot." A customer at a nearby table began waving his hand in the air.

"I better get back to work." Dot darted away and Gloria watched her friend, her heart heavy. She finished her coffee and slipped a five-dollar bill under the cup before heading out of the restaurant.

Her next stop was Nails and Knobs, Brian and Andrea's hardware store, located at the end of Belhaven's main street. Thanksgiving was right around the corner, and Paul and Gloria were finishing all of the projects they'd been working on for the Thanksgiving feast they planned to hold out in their barn.

All of the Garden Girls, with the exception of Brian and Andrea, who planned to travel to New York to be with Andrea's family, would be celebrating with them. Gloria was looking forward to a fun day full of food and fellowship, and the only dark cloud looming on the horizon was the outcome of Dot's biopsy.

Gloria climbed the steps and opened the front door, the bell tinkling merrily as she stepped inside. The hardware store was one of her favorite places; the smell of sawdust mixed with metal was familiar...comforting.

Brian was in the back, waiting on a customer and Gloria made a beeline for the display of extension cords. Paul had purchased two new portable heaters to warm the barn, but the only outlets were inside the old milking parlor.

She grabbed a couple of heavy-duty extension cords and carried them to the back to the checkout counter. "Lucy Carlson."

Lucy spun around. "Gloria. You're out early this morning."

"Paul started a new job, so I decided to get a jump on my errands." Gloria pointed at the small stack of outlet covers. "Have you started on your new reno project?"

"Yes." Lucy nodded. "We finally closed on the farm over on White Pine Trail, and it freed up some cash for our new project, which by the way, is coming along nicely."

Brian dropped the outlet covers and Lucy's receipt in the bag. "Lucy is one of my best customers these days."

"How is Margaret? I haven't seen hide nor hair of either of you for days now."

"She's good. I'm keeping her busy...grumbling, but busy," Lucy said. "Margaret doesn't have me fooled, though. She loves every minute of it."

"I'll have to run by to check it out."

Lucy explained the new project was a vacant tri-level, not far from Green Springs and then rattled off the address.

"Maybe I'll stop by later today since I'm rambling around with nothing much to do."

"Wear some old clothes and we'll put you to work." Lucy tied the handles of the plastic bag. "We'll see you later. Thanks Brian."

Gloria waited until Lucy exited the hardware store and then placed the extension cords on the counter. "We're almost ready for the Thanksgiving Day feast. Are you certain you and Andrea don't want to hang around? I'll bet New York is a circus during the holiday season."

"I'm sure it is" Brian reached for one of the cords. "We don't have a choice. Andrea doesn't want to travel after the end of this year. She's nervous about the baby and wants to make the trip sooner rather than later."

"Can't say that I blame her," Gloria said. "I was going to pop in to see how she's feeling."

"She's feeling much better, more like her old self, but she's not home. She went to Grand Rapids with Alice to check out some baby shops. There's a specific brand of crib she wants to look at." Brian shook his head. "Talk about baby fever."

Gloria smiled. "It's only natural. She's going to make a wonderful mother...you'll make wonderful parents." She chatted with Brian for a few more moments while she paid for her purchases, promising to give Andrea a call later to check on her.

She retraced her steps, back to the post office where she'd parked her car when the eerie wail of sirens echoed in the air, causing the hairs on the back of Gloria's neck to stand up.

She quickly unlocked the driver's side door and tossed her purchase inside when Ruth bolted from the post office and ran into the parking lot. "Dot called! Rose and Johnnie's house is on fire!"

Chapter 2

"Oh no!" Gloria hopped into her car.

"I'm going with you." Ruth slid into the passenger seat.

"Who's going to cover the post office?"

"Kenny is going to stick around until I get back."

"I hope Rose and Johnnie are okay." Gloria rammed the car into reverse, spinning the steering wheel as she backed up, narrowly missing Judith Arnett, who jumped out of Gloria's path.

Ruth rolled down the window and hung her head out. "Sorry Judith. Rose Morris' house is on fire!"

Judith nodded as she pressed her body against the brick building. "I hope she's okay."

Gloria shifted into gear and hit the gas a little too hard, sending a small spray of pebbles across the parking lot.

"Judith is gonna think you did that on purpose."

"I know, but it was an accident," Gloria said, as she made sure the coast was clear and careened onto Main Street. She turned left, and they sped past the red brick fire station. The overhead doors were up and the bays empty. "They took all of the fire trucks. This can't be a good sign."

"I wouldn't panic just yet. The firefighters take all of the fire trucks even if it's a burner barrel fire."

Gloria drove as fast as she dared until she rounded the curve, leading out of Belhaven. All of Belhaven's fire vehicles surrounded the Morris' one-story ranch home. She let out a small sigh of relief when she spied several of the volunteer firefighters milling about in the driveway.

15

She eased Annabelle onto the side of the road and parked behind Sally Keane's car.

They made their way over to Sally, who was standing on the edge of the driveway a safe distance from the trucks and firefighters. "Have you seen Rose and Johnnie? Are they okay?" Ruth asked.

Sally shifted her gaze. "Hi Ruth, Gloria. I don't know. By the time I got here, they were extinguishing a few flames near the back of the house. I haven't seen Johnnie or Rose."

"If I remember correctly, there's a small closet in the back corner, leading into the kitchen." Gloria started to say it was where Rose stored her special elixirs, but didn't want to give Sally Keane an ounce of ammunition to start spreading rumors.

"I see someone coming out the front door," Sally said. "It looks like Johnnie."

One of the firefighters guided Johnnie down the front steps and to the front yard.

"Dear God, please let Rose be okay," Gloria whispered.

The front door swung open and a second firefighter escorted Rose out of the home, and they joined Johnnie in the front yard.

"There's Dot." Ruth pointed to the road and they watched as Dot parked behind Gloria's car and ran to join them. "What happened?"

"We don't know yet," Ruth said. "The firefighters are with Rose and Johnnie."

Dot's hand flew to her throat. "Rose called earlier to let me know she was running a little behind. She was wrapping up a project for Ruth."

"I'm gonna see what Joe knows." Sally Keane made a beeline for Officer Joe Nelson, her on-again, off-again boyfriend.

"Ruth," Gloria turned to her friend. "Was Rose planning to bring you that special potion this morning?"

Ruth hung her head and stared at the ground. "Yes," she said in a small voice. "I had no idea it was going to, literally, blow up in her face."

"Ruth Carpenter. Does Rose's project have anything to do with you jogging on the sides of the road in the morning when I'm on my way to the restaurant?" Dot asked.

"Maybe," Ruth hedged.

Dot lifted a brow. "Spill the beans. What is going on?"

"I'm training for the elimination rounds of Dash for Cash. They're coming to Grand Rapids in a few days and I'm on the list. If I make this cut, I'm on the show." Ruth clasped her hands. "I've been applying for months and they finally contacted me. Rose has been supplying me with a special elixir she's convinced will give me an edge on the other contestants."

"It doesn't have those ster – whatever, does it?" Dot asked. "Those are dangerous."

"Steroids. I already asked. Rose swears it's a natural energy enhancer."

"Potentially flammable at that," Gloria said.

Sally Keane rejoined the trio. "Joe can't tell me much right now, other than it appears Rose was working on one of her special elixirs, something went wrong and the concoction she was cooking on the stovetop caused a small explosion and fire. Rose tried to put it out, but it somehow spread."

"Are they going to be all right?" Dot asked.

"Joe thinks so. Both she and Johnnie inhaled some of the fumes and they're complaining of feeling lightheaded and nauseous, so the firefighters are waiting to see if they need to call an ambulance."

"I wonder what exploded," Gloria murmured.

Sally shrugged. "Whatever it was, it stained the walls and Joe said the place smells like a doughnut shop."

"Let me guess, it's purple," Dot said.

"Yeah. Bright purple."

"I'm sure it's the same purple stain that has been on Rose's hands for days now, for whatever secret project she's been working on for Ruth." Dot lifted a brow.

"Don't look at me like that," Ruth said. "Rose offered to help me out. I didn't ask her."

"You wouldn't happen to know what the special purple ingredient might be, would you Ruth?" Gloria asked.

"It's butterfly pea powder and more of a blue shade than purple. I looked it up. The stuff is a legit substance. They use it to color teas and other beverages."

"I guess we'll have to wait to ask Rose what caught fire," Dot said. "Someone needs to stay behind to make sure they're all right. I have to get back to the restaurant. Everyone hightailed it out of there after hearing about the fire. Ray is all alone, holding down the fort."

"They'll all be heading there soon to discuss the incident," Gloria said. "Dot, if you could give Ruth a ride back into town, I'll stay."

"Sure." Dot jingled her van keys. "Please let us know as soon as you hear something."

"Of course." While Gloria waited, she sent text messages to Lucy, Margaret and Andrea, filling them in on the fire.

Finally, the scene began to clear as several of the firefighters climbed into their trucks and left, leaving only one fire truck and two firefighters.

One of the firefighters helped Rose to her feet and the couple stood talking while they packed up their emergency medical kits.

Gloria waited until the last fire truck drove off before hurrying across the drive.

Johnnie nodded at Gloria but never took his eyes off his wife. "I'm gonna build you a shed out back, so the next time you wanna start messing around with your hocus pocus stuff, you can blow the shed sky high."

"Rose. Johnnie. I'm glad you're okay," Gloria said. "What happened?"

"I had a minor mishap in the kitchen," Rose grumbled. "It caused a teeny amount of damage to our kitchen."

"Teeny?" Johnnie gasped. "The kitchen wall is purple and you torched one of the cabinets. I'm telling you, Rose, this is a wakeup call. One day one of your concoctions is gonna make someone sick, or worse. We'll be sued and lose everything."

"You're wrong," Rose insisted. "Aunt Lajaria used her herbal blends for years with minimal side effects. They're safer than half of the vitamins on the market."

Johnnie ignored the comment and turned to Gloria. "Did Rose tell you she started an online internet shop and is selling her hocus pocus stuff?"

"No." Although Gloria recalled Rose mentioning it on more than one occasion, especially after one of her more recent, concoctions appeared to help Eleanor Whittaker, an elderly Belhaven resident. She attempted to steer the conversation to safer ground. "I hope your home didn't suffer too much damage."

"I got a look at it before the firefighters showed up," Johnnie said. "Other than smelling like cinnamon rolls and sporting a new shade of purple..."

"Blue," Rose interrupted.

"Blue, purple, it might as well be neon green...some drywall will need to be replaced. I'm not sure about salvaging the kitchen cabinet. Rose torched it pretty good."

"How was I supposed to know cinnamon would explode?"

Johnnie sucked in a breath. "Like I said, I'm gonna build you a crack shack out back, but until I do, no more using the kitchen stove."

"I have to have heat," Rose argued.

"I'll buy you a hot plate."

Gloria tapped Rose's arm. "Hey! Look who's here."

Rose and Johnnie stopped arguing as a familiar vehicle pulled into the drive.

Chapter 3

The trio watched as Brian and Ray climbed out of the Nails and Knobs company pick-up truck and joined the trio.

"Brian and I thought we'd run by and try to shore up your kitchen, so the place is habitable," Ray said.

"I appreciate the help," Johnnie said. "The queen of concoctions decided to liven things up by setting the kitchen on fire."

Johnnie led the others into the kitchen. He pointed to the bluish purple spatters that coated one of the kitchen cabinets and the sooty wall. "I'm not sure there's much you'll be able to do with the damage to the counter and cabinet. It looks like they're permanently stained."

Brian ran his hand over the cabinet. "You're right. The cabinet and part of the counter will have to be replaced."

"I oughta leave it just like that, to remind my wife what happens when she starts mixing up her hocus pocus stuff."

Rose opened her mouth to shoot off a snappy reply and Johnnie held up a hand. "I appreciate you guys coming by to help out. While you're here, Brian, I need a quote on a 10'x10' wooden shed, something I can hook up to power. Rose is moving her goodies out of the house."

"That remains to be seen," Rose mumbled.

"I have to admit it does smell good in here," Ray said. "Like cinnamon rolls."

"It could be worse," Gloria said.

"Oh, it has been," Johnnie said. "Like the time Rose was working on a new formula and it smelled like cow manure in here for weeks."

Ray and Brian made quick work of installing a couple of sheets of drywall and applying a coat of drywall mud before they packed up their tools and carried them to Brian's truck. "I better head back to the restaurant. Dot is feeling a little under the weather. I called Holly in to help out so that she could go home and get some rest."

"I appreciate the help guys. And I promise if I have my way, it won't happen again." Johnnie gave his wife a hard stare.

Gloria remembered Dot's earlier admission about the biopsy. "If you need a couple of extra helping hands down at the restaurant, Paul is working in Rockville and I have plenty of time to pitch in and help out."

"Thanks Gloria. We may take you up on that." Ray gave Gloria a sad smile and then shuffled to the truck, his shoulders hunched.

"I need to get going, too." Gloria said.

"I'll walk you out." Rose grabbed her sweater off the hook and accompanied Gloria to her car.

She waited until her friend was inside before leaning in. "You gotta give this to Ruth."

Rose shoved a small plastic pouch into Gloria's hand. "This is my super-powered next level brew. Tell her to mix one eighth teaspoon with her tea. It has to be green tea and the tea has to be hot, almost boiling. I haven't finished testing it yet, but from what I do know, the effectiveness will only last for a few hours."

"I thought..." Gloria's voice trailed off as she stared at the purplish powder.

"I finished the first batch, no problem. It was the second batch that caught fire. Now tell her if she's careful, this should last her through both rounds of the competition."

"What about Johnnie?"

"Ah." Rose waved a hand. "I can handle my husband. Remember an eighth of a teaspoon in piping hot green tea."

"Got it." Gloria gave Rose two thumbs up and then backed out of the driveway before returning to the post office parking lot. She shut the car off and then slipped the pouch into her purse before heading inside. The place was packed, and Gloria guessed all of the area residents were discussing the Morris' fire.

She zigzagged past several patrons and approached the counter, where Ruth stood talking to Judith Arnett. "Hello Judith. I'm sorry about earlier. I didn't mean to almost run you over – or spray you with rocks."

"Hi Gloria. It's okay." Judith shifted to the right. "Ruth and I were discussing the Morris' fire. I'm glad to hear Rose and Johnnie are okay." She rattled on about the dangers of Rose's potions, how she thought Rose needed to submit them to the FDA for approval. "This black market selling could really backfire on Rose if she's not careful."

Gloria wasn't sure if Judith was hinting she planned to turn Rose in. She hoped not. Although she wasn't completely convinced Rose was aware of how potentially dangerous her concoctions could be.

"Eleanor swears by Rose's elixirs and I have to admit, she seems much more peppy and full of vigor these days. I love her yoga classes." Judith glanced at her watch. "Speaking of that, I better get going. Eleanor doesn't like it when we're late."

Gloria waited until Judith exited the post office before turning her attention to Ruth. "Thank goodness Rose and Johnnie are all right." She reached inside her purse, pulled out the blue packet and slid it across the counter. "Rose said to give you this. You're to mix one eighth teaspoon in hot - piping hot - green tea."

"Sweet!" Ruth snatched the packet off the counter and dropped it into her uniform pocket. "I thought the elimination rounds wouldn't be until next week, but I just got an email. The first round of eliminations is at nine tomorrow morning. Kenny is gonna cover here for me. What are you doing tomorrow?"

"Tomorrow? I don't know," Gloria said. "Why?"

"I could use a little moral support and was thinking since Paul was working that you might have time to go with me. Kenny can't go. Someone has to stay here."

"I...sure. What time will we have to leave?"

"Early," Ruth said. "I say if we leave by seven, it should give us plenty of time to get to the convention center by nine."

On the one hand, Gloria wasn't much of an early bird. On the other, she would already be up to see Paul off. It also wouldn't hurt for someone to keep an eye on Ruth. "Okay. I'll meet you here at seven."

"Thanks Gloria. I have a good feeling about this. I think I'm gonna make it through the elimination round with flying colors."

"I hope you do, Ruth." Gloria told her friend good-bye and then headed out of the post office, silently hoping she wouldn't be too disappointed if she didn't make the cut.

***

Gloria tapped on the back door of the post office at 7:00 a.m. on the dot.

Ruth appeared in the doorway. "You're right on time."

"Do you want me to drive?"

"No. I put my mini-microwave in the van, so that I could heat the tea and mix Rose's brew before we get to the convention center. I thought about mixing it and putting it in a Thermos, but Rose said it needed to be piping hot." Ruth reached for the door handle. "See you later Kenny."

Kenny dropped the mail on the counter and met them at the door. "Good luck Ruth. You got this. Don't let the Mahoney woman get under your skin."

"Yeah, well she better watch out. I'm sick of her snide comments," Ruth growled. She thanked Kenny and then followed Gloria to the van.

Gloria hopped into the passenger seat and reached for the seatbelt. "Who is Mahoney?" She thought the name sounded familiar, but couldn't place it.

"Amy Mahoney is one of the other contestants trying out for the show. She's a member of our online chat group and has been bragging about how she's got this in the bag, and the rest of us don't stand a chance."

Ruth started the van and shifted into reverse. "I quoted her one of your favorite sayings - 'pride goeth before the fall.' She didn't like that, and we started exchanging a few un-pleasantries."

Ruth pulled the van onto the street. "She's a real gem. I can tell her one thing...she doesn't want to mess with Ruth Carpenter."

Gloria said the first thing that popped into her head. "It will all be over soon." She wasn't sure how Ruth would react if she didn't make the cut. In Gloria's opinion she was taking the contest a little too seriously and hoped her friend wouldn't be disappointed with the outcome.

During the long ride, they chatted about Thanksgiving, about Rose and Johnnie's fire, about Andrea and Brian's baby and then the conversation drifted back to the contest. "Can you start warming the tea? We're getting kinda close. The microwave is sitting on the back seat."

Gloria reached behind her and grabbed the edge of the small appliance. She tugged it towards her, balancing it in her left hand and then eased it onto her lap.

"The converter is in here." Ruth tapped the top of her center console.

"I've never seen a portable microwave for a vehicle. I guess if you were forced to move out of your house, you could live in your van." Gloria popped the lid on the van's center console and peered inside.

"I haven't used the converter in a while. It might be buried in the bottom."

Gloria stuck her hand inside, the tips of her fingers making contact with a glob of fuzz. "What in the world? There's something fuzzy in here." She pinched the fuzz between her fingers and pulled out a grayish-glob, covered in a thick layer of white mold. "Disgusting."

Ruth gave the object a quick glance. "That's my pickle." She plucked it from Gloria's hand, rolled the driver's side window down and tossed it out. "I wondered what happened to it."

"How did a pickle end up in the bottom of your console?" Gloria wiped the tips of her fingers on the front of her slacks.

"It was during a recent stakeout. Kenny has a new girlfriend and he wanted me to spy..."

"Uh." Gloria held up her hand. "I don't think I want to know." She rifled through the rest of the console, this time keeping an eye on what she was reaching for, and finally found the converter, the side of it sticky. "It appears the pickle and your converter bonded."

She shoved the charger into the socket and then grasped the microwave plug-in. "I'm not going to get electrocuted, am I?"

"Nah. I've used this dozens of times," Ruth said. "The tea is ready to go. All you need to do is warm it up."

"Here goes nothing," Gloria mumbled. "Maybe you should've let me do the driving instead."

"You mean drive my van?" Ruth gasped.

"True. Scratch that." The only way Ruth would allow someone to drive her van was if she was unconscious.

Gloria jabbed the express one-minute button and her lap hummed while the microwave warmed the tea. After it finished warming, Gloria gingerly removed the steaming cup and handed it to her friend. "Be careful. It's hot."

"Thanks." Ruth balanced the cup in one hand, her eyes never leaving the road. "The cinnamon is a nice touch. I still feel guilty about Rose's kitchen."

"Don't be too hard on yourself. I have a feeling from what Johnnie said, this isn't the first time something went awry with Rose's concoctions."

The women rode in silence for several long moments. Gloria didn't want to distract Ruth from focusing on the road, and as they got close to Grand Rapids, the traffic became heavy. Despite the congested roads, they reached the convention center with fifteen minutes to spare.

Ruth eased into an empty parking spot and shut the van off before downing the rest of her tea. "I'm feeling more energized by the minute."

"That's good." Gloria reached for her purse. "Do you have any idea what types of elimination rounds you'll be competing in?"

"Not a clue. A couple of contestants from Indiana, who tried out last week said there was an obstacle course, a balancing beam routine and even one where the contestants had to consume a variety of spicy foods in less than a minute."

"That one wouldn't be for me." Gloria clutched her stomach. "I'm ready when you are."

Ruth grabbed a backpack from the back seat as Gloria glanced around. The parking lot was almost full, and she wondered if all of the vehicles belonged to people who were trying out for the show.

Ruth and Gloria entered the building and joined the registration line. When they reached the front, Gloria stood off to the side while Ruth approached a man seated behind the desk. He consulted his clipboard before handing her a bib number. Ruth peeled the backing off and slapped it on the front of her shirt.

Next, he handed her a raincoat. Ruth nodded enthusiastically and then hurried to join Gloria. "I'm in the second string of contestants. It should be about an hour before they call my name and number."

"Where do we go?"

"This way." Ruth pointed to a large set of double doors. "First, I gotta tinkle...all that tea."

The women headed to the restrooms, and after finishing up, they made their way into the large auditorium. Folding chairs lined one wall. To the right were large room dividers, and to the left was a padded floor mat. A retractable belt barrier surrounded the mat. "Let's stand near the back, so we can scope out the competition," Ruth whispered.

"Lead the way." Gloria followed her friend to the back of the seating area and stood in the corner while Ruth paced back and forth, studying the other contestants. On her third pass, Gloria stopped her. "You're making me dizzy, just watching you."

"Sorry," Ruth said. "I'm nervous as a tic, not to mention Rose's potion has me wound up tighter than a top."

"Did they explain to you what you're doing for the first round of eliminations?"

"Yeah." Ruth waved the raincoat she was holding. "After we put these raincoats on, they're going to spray the outside with vegetable oil. We then make our way inside the roped-in area. When all of the contestants are inside the ring and the buzzer sounds, we have to swipe the other contestants' tags off the back of the jackets. The last five contestants to have their tags still intact snag a spot on the show, but there's one more round. In my opinion, the final competition is even more important than the first."

"How so?"

"The top two to finish, get to pick the Dash for Cash game show contests and they don't have to tell the others what they are," Ruth said. "It's a definite advantage because they'll have time to hone their skills."

"What...is the second round?" Gloria's eyes wandered to the tall dividers.

"The winners will be blindfolded and they have to navigate their way through the makeshift maze. It'll be a piece of cake. I'm used to working in the dark."

"True."

The longer they waited, the more concerned Gloria became. She was worried about the tussle for tags. Despite Rose's special elixir, Ruth was no spring chicken, and several of the contestants were decades younger. A few reminded Gloria of bodybuilders and trainers, who would have no problem competing against a 60-something woman, even if she was in tip-top shape.

41

The first round of contestants to compete in the tag elimination offered Ruth a chance to map her strategy.

"Are you sure you want to do this?" Gloria asked.

"Positive." Ruth slipped her backpack off and held it out. "Can you hang onto this for me?"

"Of course."

Finally, the second group of contestants, including Ruth, entered the roped-in area and Gloria clenched her fists. The buzzer sounded and Ruth dove for a nearby contestant's tag, easily ripping it off.

Despite Gloria's concerns, Ruth held her own, and when the buzzer sounded and the competition officially ended, she was still standing, tag intact.

Gloria grinned as she watched Ruth whip the raincoat off and march toward the exit. Her excitement for her friend turned to disbelief as one of the other contestants, a young woman, clotheslined Ruth, knocking her flat on her back.

Chapter 4

The crowd gasped as Ruth lay there unmoving while Gloria shoved past several spectators and ran to the ropes. By the time she got there, Ruth was sitting upright. "Ruth! Are you okay?"

"Yeah," Ruth rubbed the side of her neck. "That witch Mahoney tried to take me out."

One of the referees climbed into the ring and helped Ruth to her feet. "What happened?"

"One of the other contestants clotheslined me. It was the Mahoney chick."

Another referee joined the first, and the two men escorted Ruth off to the side.

The trio talked in low voices, and then the referees walked away.

Gloria stepped to Ruth's side. "I hope they disqualify the person who knocked you down."

"I thought they would, too. I have a feeling Mahoney has connections. The refs kept saying something about how their hands were tied. I hope this whole thing isn't rigged and I'm not wasting my time."

"Try not to let it get you down. Besides, they need more than one contestant, and you made it to the second round, fair and square."

"True." Ruth brightened. "Did you see me out there? I was taking out people half my age."

"You were awesome Ruth. It was fun to watch."

The women headed to a concession stand where Gloria ordered two coffees and some pastries, thinking Ruth might need a little extra sugar to carry her through the next round.

The seating area was packed, and the women finally found an empty table in the back. Gloria set one of the coffees in front of Ruth, lifted her cup and eyed her friend over the rim. "Do you have a strategy for making it in the top two of the maze competition?"

"Nah. I tried to study the pattern, but there's a thick net covering the top and I can't figure out which way it zigs and zags." Ruth stared at the array of donuts. "Those look good, but I've got something better." She unzipped her backpack and pulled out a green Bentgo lunch box, snapped the latch and lifted the lid. "I've been on a strict high protein, high energy diet."

Inside the box were boiled eggs and a compartment filled with almonds. Next to the almonds was a glob of white. "What is that?"

"Plain yogurt. Check it out." Ruth reached into the backpack a second time and pulled out a small container of honey. She peeled the top off and drizzled the honey on top of the yogurt. "Hand me one of those spoons."

Gloria handed Ruth a disposable spoon and watched as she swirled the honey around the yogurt. She grabbed a handful of almonds and sprinkled them on top. "Wanna try a bite?"

"No." Gloria shook her head. "It's all yours."

Ruth ladled a heaping spoonful and started to eat. "I'm gonna have to keep an eye on that Mahoney woman, although it might be a little tough blindfolded. I wouldn't put it past her to attack me again."

The women discussed strategy as they sipped their coffee and ate the food. During the chat, Ruth reminded Gloria she and Amy Mahoney had exchanged heated words in the chat group. "Did I tell you she works for UPS? Somehow, she's convinced that working for UPS makes her better than a United States Postal Service employee. The woman is nothing but a bag of hot air. In fact, she's motivating me to make sure I make it to the end before her. I would love to rub it in her face."

"Bless those who curse you. Pray for those who hurt you."

"I know, I know," Ruth said. "I'll be glad when it's over and I don't have to see Mahoney again until the game show, which reminds me; I gotta run out to the van for a minute and grab my blood pressure medicine. It's in the glove box."

By the time Ruth returned, the speakers overhead began to blare, informing the final round of contestants that it was time to make their way to the maze's entrance.

"I'll take care of the food," Gloria said. "Now all you gotta do is kick Mahoney's butt."

"I'll settle for the top two."

As Ruth walked away, a sense of foreboding filled Gloria. It was bad enough that all of the contestants were blindfolded; wandering around aimlessly inside the maze, but even worse the spectators had no idea what was going on. Even the referees and officials had no overhead visual since the top of the maze was covered with a thick layer of netting.

Gloria reached the viewing area as the buzzer sounded and the contestants inched forward, jockeying for position before they disappeared from sight.

The sides of the structure began to shake and the crowd began to murmur. Gloria squeezed her eyes shut, waiting for one of the portable walls to hit the floor and the contestants to tumble out like a stack of dominoes.

The emcee kept up a light banter as the crowd waited for the first contestant to exit the maze. "This certainly is a nail-biter, folks. Can you hear the grunts and groans? Maybe we should've put them in knee and elbow pads."

The comment got the appropriate amount of chuckles from the crowd and for the umpteenth time, Gloria wondered why on earth Ruth decided she wanted to be a contestant on Dash for Cash. It wasn't as if she needed the money. Her job at the post office was one of the best jobs in the area.

Ruth could work as long as she wanted, until she was ready to retire.

Maybe Ruth was bored. She thought of Lucy and Margaret's rehab projects. Dot and Rose stayed busy at the restaurant. Andrea and Brian had their hands full with three businesses, not to mention a baby on the way.

It was a tense twenty minutes before the first contestant emerged. He tore his blindfold off and pumped his fists in the air triumphantly. Right behind him was a woman, and she followed suit, jumping up and down.

The third was close behind and there was still no sign of Ruth. It seemed like forever before Ruth finally emerged, and Gloria released the breath she was holding.

She shifted her attention to the other contestants. Ruth's nemesis, Mahoney, wasn't one of them and had yet to exit the maze. Two of the officials hovered near the exit, waiting for the woman to emerge.

Another of the officials joined them and they huddled together, Gloria guessed to try to figure out what they should do. Finally, one of them broke from the group and entered the maze.

Moments later, several workers disappeared inside.

The other contestants, unaware of the unfolding event, gathered around the emcee, who handed each of them a packet. Gloria watched as Ruth tucked the packet under her arm, her eyes searching the seating area.

Gloria waved and Ruth made her way over.

"You did it. Oh my gosh Ruth. I would've freaked out, being blindfolded and wandering around, trying to find my way out, not to mention running into those other people, who were also trying to get out."

"It was a tight situation," Ruth admitted. "For a minute there, I thought I was headed in the wrong direction. When I crossed the finish line and heard the emcee call number four, I almost threw up."

"What happened to Amy Mahoney?"

Ruth frowned. "I don't know. I was so excited for the maze phase to end, I forgot all about her."

Gloria told Ruth how the officials stood near the exit, one went inside and the rest followed shortly after.

"That's odd."

Gloria pointed at the packet. "What's next?"

"These are the contest rules and regulations. I thought I was gonna get a free trip to New York for the show's taping, but they're changing it up, and the contest will be held at an undisclosed location here in Grand Rapids."

"That's even better," Gloria said. "You know all of the girls will want to come watch."

"True. I hadn't thought of that." Ruth glanced at the group of people gathering near the exit. "I wonder what's going on. It must have something to do with Mahoney."

Gloria and Ruth joined the crowd, hovering off to the side to watch when several uniformed police officers, followed by EMTs, stormed into the hall.

"This can't be good," Gloria said. "Let's see if we can get a closer look."

The women circled the maze until they spotted a gap in the wall where they caught a glimpse of a woman lying on the floor.

Chapter 5

"It's Mahoney," Ruth whispered. "Maybe she knocked herself out, running into a corner of the maze."

The theory quickly flew out the window when Gloria overheard one of the medical technicians tell his partner the woman's pulse was weak. The technician leaned over Amy Mahoney's still form and began checking her vitals.

"Okay folks. You're gonna have to move back." One of the center's security guards began waving his arms, motioning them to step back. "There's nothing to see."

Ruth grabbed Gloria's arm and pulled her off to the side. "I didn't want Amy Mahoney to beat me out of the maze, but I certainly didn't want her to get hurt."

"Maybe she had a heart attack," Gloria theorized. "I mean, this whole contest competition was stressful for me, and I wasn't even a participant."

"Yeah. It was harder than I thought. I'm sure we'll hear more about what happened on the news."

When they reached the van, Ruth unlocked the doors and Gloria slid onto the passenger seat. She waited until her friend pulled onto the highway before talking. "What's the verdict?"

"Verdict?"

"On Rose's potion. Do you think it helped you win?"

"I dunno. I was running on 100% adrenaline, although it may have been self-induced. It sure didn't hurt." Ruth tightened her grip on the steering wheel. "All that physical exertion made me hungry. Let's stop by a burger joint on our way to Belhaven. Don't tell Kenny, though. He'll freak out if he finds out I'm eating fast food."

After a quick trip through the drive through, the women were once again on the road. "Thanks for tagging along."

"You're welcome. I had fun watching you." Gloria took a bite of burger and chewed thoughtfully. "Do you have any idea how many tags you ripped off in the first competition?"

"At least five. The greasy film on the raincoat made it hard to grab hold of the tags. Once I did, though, there was no stopping me." Ruth shoved a French fry in her mouth. "I hate to speak ill of the woman, but Amy Mahoney was trying to cheat. I swear she tried to trip me twice inside the ring before she finally clotheslined me."

"Did she say anything to you?" Gloria asked.

"Not during the first competition. When we got to the maze, we were all blindfolded and right before the buzzer went off, I could've sworn I heard Amy say something to me."

"What?"

"You're both going down."

Gloria frowned. "That's an odd thing to say. Who is 'both'?"

Ruth shrugged. "I thought maybe she was talking about you, but that doesn't make sense. Why would you be a threat? You weren't even competing."

"Maybe she believed you were friends with one of the other contestants." Gloria shifted the conversation to the upcoming game show and then back to the Thanksgiving dinner.

When they reached the post office, Ruth parked her van in an empty spot in the employee parking lot and climbed out.

Gloria joined her near the back of the building. "I don't want to steal your thunder. This is your moment of glory and your story to tell. I'm going to head home before anyone can ask how it went."

"Thanks Gloria." Ruth grinned. "I guess Kenny and I will have to ramp up my training."

"When will you be competing on Dash for Cash?"

"They're taping it on the Tuesday before Thanksgiving, so I don't have much time," Ruth said.

Gloria waited until her friend slipped inside the back of the post office before climbing into her car and heading home.

It was still early, and Gloria had several hours before Paul arrived home, so she decided to experiment with a slow cooker chicken barbecue recipe she'd found online. The recipe was simple and she had all of the ingredients on hand.

After reading the reviews, she decided to "tweak" the recipe by adding chopped yellow onions to the bottom of the crockpot. Next, she minced some fresh garlic and sprinkled it on top of the onions before placing several boneless chicken breasts in the pot.

She turned the crockpot on high and set the kitchen timer for two hours.

Gloria's son, Eddie and his wife, Karen, planned to spend Thanksgiving with Paul and her. The bedroom they would be staying in needed a little dusting and freshening up, so she headed upstairs.

Thankfully, Gloria and her friends had held a large barn sale some time back, and all of the decades of accumulated stuff was gone. She ran a feather duster over the dressers before gathering up the sheets and blankets to throw in the washer.

While she worked, she thought of Amy Mahoney. The woman appeared to be young. Perhaps the stress of the competition had triggered an unforeseen medical event.

Gloria descended the steps and tossed the bedding into the washing machine before wandering to the dining room and settling in at the computer. Despite downsizing their garden, Paul and she had harvested bushels of fruits and veggies, and Gloria was determined to find a few new recipes for the Thanksgiving Day meal.

After researching the recipes and printing off a couple that looked promising, she checked her email account and then played an online mystery mansion game until the timer for the crockpot went off.

She removed the chicken breasts and set them off to the side to cool. While the chicken cooled, she mixed a large bottle of barbecue sauce and some Italian dressing together.

Next, she shredded the chicken and dumped it back into the crockpot. She poured the sauce on top and stirred it before replacing the lid.

Mally, who sat patiently watching Gloria mix the ingredients, began thumping her tail.

"Would you like to go out?" Gloria grabbed her sweater and the two of them headed to the porch. "Perhaps it's time for a trip to the creek." They made it as far as the bottom of the steps when a yellow jeep swung into the drive.

Lucy gave a jaunty wave before springing from the jeep. "I hoped I would catch you at home.

Margaret and I both had some errands to take care of, so we knocked off early today."

"Mally and I were getting ready to head back to the creek. Would you like to join us?"

"Sure. Let me grab my jacket." Lucy reached inside the jeep. "I swung by the post office on my way here to ask Ruth how the contest went. It looks like she's gonna be on Dash for Cash."

"Yeah. She's pumped. Have you stopped by the restaurant to talk to Rose about her fire?"

"Not yet." Lucy shook her head. "Ruth said that Johnnie ordered a shed from Brian and is insisting that Rose start using it for mixing her elixirs."

"It's probably not a bad idea. I'm not sure if Rose's potion worked for Ruth. It sure didn't hurt." The women wandered along a grassy patch while Lucy updated her on the new renovation project. "I think after we finish this one, we're going take a break for a couple of months. Margaret wants to spend Christmas in

Albuquerque with Chad. This will be her first Thanksgiving and Christmas without Don, and she doesn't want to be home to face the holidays alone."

Don, Margaret's husband, had died earlier in the year, leaving Margaret and the whole town of Belhaven in shock at his sudden death. It had taken months for Margaret to start to come around, thanks to Lucy's new business endeavor, Hip Chick Flips. The women had successfully flipped one home and were working on their second.

"That's a great idea. She'll be here with us for Thanksgiving, so I'll be sure to keep her busy helping me," Gloria promised. "What about you? I haven't heard you mention Max Field in weeks."

Gloria and Lucy had met Max during the investigation into Milton Tilton's disappearance. The two had hit it off and started dating.

Lucy wrinkled her nose. "It's over. I mean, Max and I are still friends. I think he felt threatened by my new business and even hinted around that women weren't supposed to run construction businesses. It was a man's line of work. Can you believe the nerve? I finally told him I had my hands full running my reno business and didn't have a lot of free time to invest in our relationship, but that we could still be friends."

She continued. "Not only that, he kept pushing to move our relationship to the next level and I'm not ready. I may never be ready, if that makes sense."

It made perfect sense to Gloria. She remembered how, although she'd been lonely after her first husband, James, passed away, the last thing she'd been looking for was a romantic relationship, but God had other plans and put Paul directly in her path.

She was thankful he had, and Gloria loved her husband with all of her heart, but it wasn't something she'd sought out. "It makes perfect sense. Maybe someday you'll change your mind. If you're content with your life the way it is and you don't feel like you're missing anything, then don't force it."

"My sentiments exactly," Lucy agreed. "I've been so busy; I haven't even had a chance to scope out my blinds for deer hunting this year."

"Oh no." Gloria chuckled and shook her head. "As much as I love you, Lucy, I have no plans to go deer hunting this year."

"Are you sure? I mean, think of all of the venison we could put in your freezer. Free meat."

"Why don't you ask Margaret instead?"

"Margaret won't go. You should have seen the look on her face when I told her I was thinking of building a chicken coop and raising a few chickens."

"You are? Don't let my grandson, Ryan, hear you say that. He's been bugging me for months now to get farm animals. His logic is if I live on a farm, I need animals."

"Chickens aren't hard," Lucy argued.

"You get the chickens and I'll buy eggs from you...and venison if you get a buck this year."

"You're no fun."

Mally, who had gone ahead, waited patiently near the wooded area for Gloria to give her the okay. "All right Mally. You can go check out the creek."

The trees were bare, and the fallen leaves crunched under the women's feet as they trailed behind Mally and made their way to the edge of the creek.

Gloria knelt down and dipped her fingers in the cool, clear water. "The Farmer's Almanac is predicting a long, hard winter."

"I read the same thing. We've had some easy winters these past few years. I guess we're long overdue."

Gloria dried her fingers on the corner of her sweatshirt and then made her way over to a pile of logs. She perched on the edge and patted an empty spot next to her. Lucy, who was typically agile, took her time settling in next to her best friend.

"Are you feeling okay?"

"Yeah," Lucy said. "Margaret and I were trying to lug the old hot water heater out of the basement of our flip project, and I think I pulled a muscle." She began rubbing her lower back. "We finally got it out, but we decided to have the new one installed."

"We're not spring chickens anymore," Gloria said.

"Bite your tongue."

The women watched Mally frolic in the chilly creek and after the pooch tired of splashing in the water, she trotted to the log and promptly shook off, pelting them with drops of cold water. "Oh. She does it every time." Gloria swiped at the

66

droplets on her face. "Sorry Lucy. I guess that's our signal to head back."

Gloria scooched off the log and the women followed Mally out of the woods. "Would you like to stay for coffee?"

"Coffee sounds good. I already finished my errands. I was thinking of running to Dot's for dinner."

"You can hang around and eat with Paul and me. I'm trying a new recipe for slow cooker barbecue chicken."

"I don't want to impose." Lucy waited for Gloria to step inside the kitchen and then followed her in.

"You're not imposing. I'm inviting."

The tantalizing aroma of garlic and onion filled the kitchen and Gloria's stomach growled. "I think it's done." She stepped over to the counter and lifted the lid on the crockpot. Fragrant steam rose from the pot. "I think we should try a small sample." She reached into the cupboard, pulled out two salad plates and scooped a spoonful of meat onto each of the plates.

"I'll grab forks." Lucy knew the layout of her friend's kitchen as well as her own, and she headed to the silverware drawer while Gloria carried the plates to the kitchen table. "There's fresh lemonade in the fridge."

"I'll pour some." Lucy poured the lemonade while Gloria grabbed a handful of paper towels.

Lucy lifted the plate and sniffed. "This smells delicious." She stabbed a piece of meat with her fork and lifted it to her mouth. "I need this recipe."

"It's super easy." Gloria rattled off the list of ingredients as she sampled her portion. "This will make great leftovers for Paul's lunch. Now that he's working at the mall through the holiday season, I don't know what I'm going to do for the next few weeks."

"You can help Margaret and me. The entire interior of the new rehab project needs to be painted."

"Painting is my passion." Gloria stabbed the last sliver of chicken and began chewing. "Seriously, I'd love to help. I also offered to help out at Dot's Restaurant."

"Business has picked up at the restaurant since Belhaven Corners opened," Lucy said. "I thought Dot and Ray were ready to move forward with purchasing the empty building next to the restaurant until Ray called the other day and said they wanted to hold off on doing anything else for a week or so."

Gloria's heart plummeted as she remembered Dot's mention of her recent biopsy. "I'm sure they'll get back with you in a day or two." She slid her chair back and glanced at the clock. "Paul should be home soon. I think baked potatoes would make a perfect side dish."

"I'm on it." Lucy headed to the pantry, pulled three potatoes from the sack on the floor and carried them to the kitchen sink while Gloria set the table.

Mally scrambled to her feet and headed to the porch door. "Paul is here." Gloria's pooch was the unofficial door guard, and they never had to worry that someone would sneak up on them, at least not when Mally was around.

"Hello Mally." Paul eased through the doorway and patted Mally's head. "Hi Lucy." He sniffed the air. "Something smells delicious."

"It's barbecue chicken." Gloria bounced on her tiptoes and kissed her husband. "I'm trying a new recipe."

"I'm starving. Let me go wash up." Paul wandered out of the kitchen and by the time he returned, the women had finished setting the table.

Gloria poured a third glass of lemonade and set it next to Paul's plate. "How was your first day on the job?"

"Whew." Paul rolled his eyes. "The mall was a zoo. You'd think they were giving stuff away."

"And I can imagine it's only going to get worse," Gloria said.

During dinner, the trio discussed Ruth's quest to become a Dash for Cash contestant and then Lucy and Margaret's new renovation project.

They had just finished eating and began clearing the table when Mally let out a low growl and trotted to the porch door. "Is someone here?"

Paul peered into the darkness and then reached for the door handle. "It's Ruth." He held the door and Ruth stepped into the kitchen. "I'm sorry to bother you guys."

Gloria could count on one hand the number of times Ruth had stopped by unannounced. "Is everything all right?"

Ruth wrinkled her nose. "You're never gonna believe who stopped by the post office right before closing time."

"Who?"

"The police. They were there to question me about Amy Mahoney's murder."

Chapter 6

"She died?" Gloria gasped. "Someone killed her?" She motioned Ruth to the kitchen table and pulled out a chair. "How? I mean. There were people all over the place."

"Yes, there were people all over the place, but only a handful inside the maze," Ruth pointed out. "Not to mention we were all blindfolded."

"Did the authorities give any indication as to the cause of death?" Paul asked.

"Overdose. Amy died on the way to the hospital."

Gloria's hand flew to her throat. "Surely, someone heard or saw something."

"The theory is someone backed Mahoney into a dead end section of the maze and then injected her with a lethal dose of morphine."

"Maybe she killed herself," Lucy said. "Why are they questioning you?"

"Amy Mahoney and I exchanged un-pleasantries in our online chat group and right after the first competition ended this morning, she clotheslined me, knocking me flat on my back."

"This is awful," Gloria whispered. "So the police consider all of the show's contestants to be suspects?"

"Yep, and I'm suspect number one," Ruth said grimly. "Something smells good."

"It's barbecue chicken." Gloria sprang from her chair. "Have you eaten? Let me fix you a sandwich."

"I don't want to impose," Ruth said.

"You sound like Lucy." Gloria fixed Ruth a sandwich, added a handful of potato chips and set the plate in front of her friend.

"I need your help," Ruth said. "If the game show officials think I had anything to do with Mahoney's death, they're going to disqualify me from playing Dash for Cash."

"That should be the least of your worries," Lucy said.

"I know I'm not guilty. I didn't kill her." Ruth took a big bite of sandwich. "This is delicious," she mumbled.

Gloria watched Ruth eat her food, all the while her head was spinning. "Are they questioning all of the contestants that were there today, or just the ones who were in the maze?"

"They're not telling me squat, but my guess would be only those of us who were in the maze at the time of her attack." Ruth reached for a chip and broke off a piece as she eyed Gloria. "So? Are you going to help me out?"

Gloria slowly nodded. "Was there ever any doubt?"

***

"The authorities told you Amy Mahoney died of a lethal overdose injection of morphine. How do they know she didn't ingest the drug of her own free will?" Gloria asked.

"I don't think they're ruling anything out. They found a syringe lying next to her body."

"It's possible she did herself in," Lucy pointed out. "Isn't there video footage of the inside of the maze?"

"I asked the authorities the same thing," Ruth said. "Visual and audio equipment are essential in any investigation, particularly an operation as large as a game show. With contestants running around inside a maze blindfolded, they would want to make sure they could keep an eye on everyone."

Paul cleared his throat. "What did they say when you asked them about it?"

"That there was video footage, but they weren't releasing any information on what was found on the tape."

"My guess is they don't know." Gloria drummed her fingers on the table. "If they had anything concrete, they wouldn't be after you."

Ruth shoved the rest of the sandwich in her mouth and licked her fingers. "I was thinking the same thing." She tapped the top of her watch. "Which is why I purchased this ASW300 audio spy watch. The one button recording feature, combined with sixty minutes of audio recording should give us something to go on."

Gloria snorted. "You recorded the maze competition using a spy watch?"

"No, I recorded *both* the elimination round and the second competition using my spy watch. I haven't had a chance to study them yet. I don't think the visual for the tag elimination will show anything since I had to wear the raincoat and it covered the watch. Our only hope is that we'll be able to glean some clues from the maze phase."

"Ruth Carpenter." Lucy shook her head. "I shouldn't be surprised."

Ruth removed the watch and turned it over. "I almost didn't buy this baby. It set me back close to three-hundred bucks, but now I'm glad I did." She shifted her gaze. "The watch screen is too small for all of us to look at. I can run a cable from the watch to your computer so we'll have a larger visual."

Gloria wrinkled her nose. "I'm not sure if I have a cable that will work."

"I have the USB cable. It came with the watch." Ruth fumbled around in her purse and pulled out a cable.

"Let me clean up the kitchen and then we can hook your watch up to the computer in the dining room." Gloria reached for a dirty plate.

"You go ahead," Paul said. "I can clean up."

"Thanks Paul." Gloria kissed her husband on the cheek and then led her friends into the dining room where she fired up her computer and then motioned Ruth to sit.

Ruth carefully placed the watch on the desk. She plugged the cable into the side of the watch and the other end into the computer. "Like I said, I haven't had a chance to view the video yet, so I'm not sure how much we'll be able to see."

The sound of muffled voices echoed from the speakers and Gloria could've sworn she heard her voice. "Is that my voice?"

"Yeah. I was testing it while we were waiting for my name to be called for the first competition." Ruth enlarged the screen and leaned back. Gloria's face appeared.

"Isn't it illegal to record someone without their permission?" Lucy asked.

"It's a gray area, and depends on a variety of circumstances," Ruth said. "Let's just say it's an area I haven't researched thoroughly. Ignorance is bliss."

The screen moved from a shot of Gloria to the auditorium. It was apparent that a few times, Ruth forgot she was recording because the recording bounced all over, making it difficult to watch.

"It's making me dizzy," Lucy said.

"Sorry. I forgot for a minute the watch was recording," Ruth said. The video ended and then picked up again when Ruth was inside the roped-in area. The video zoomed in on a small portion of the arena.

"There she is," Ruth jabbed her finger on the screen. "Amy Mahoney. Check it out. She's looking my way."

Sure enough, the younger woman was scowling at Ruth. A loud buzzer sounded and then the camera went wild, from the floor to the ceiling, bouncing all over.

"That upped my dizziness." Gloria closed her eyes. "Tell me when it's over."

She opened her eyes and stared into the kitchen where Paul was loading the dishwasher. He caught his wife's eye and chuckled.

"It's over," Ruth announced.

"Not quite," Lucy said. "The Mahoney woman is coming toward you."

Whump. Their next visual was of the auditorium ceiling.

"And that's when the witch, God rest her soul, clotheslined me," Ruth said. The screen went blank before picking up again when one of the tan walls of the maze came into view.

The trio leaned forward and studied the footage. The recording bounced around for about a minute before leveling off. Gloria could hear heavy breathing as Ruth moved through the maze. "Is that you breathing?"

"Yeah."

"You sound like you're out of breath," Lucy said. "Like you were running."

Ruth frowned. "Yeah, well you'd be out of breath, too, if you were blindfolded and hurrying through a maze trying to be one of the top two out the other end."

"Why were there two competitions?" Lucy asked.

"In the first round, the tag elimination, the last five contestants to still have their tags affixed were guaranteed a spot on the show. The second competition was an advantage competition. The first two to make it out of the maze were given the chance to hand pick the Dash for Cash competitions."

"Did you make it in the top two?"

"I was dead last...er, I mean second to the last. Technically, Mahoney was last."

"I see...I think," Lucy said. "It's a shame we can't slow the video."

"Your wish is my command." Ruth tapped the mouse and the video began playing in slow motion. A shadowy image flitted to the right of Ruth.

"There she is," Ruth said. "Mahoney passed me one minute into the maze competition."

The screen continued to move in slow motion. Ruth bumped into the cloth wall and bounced off, teetering back and forth before regaining her balance. "I can't believe you did this, Ruth," Lucy said. "What exactly are you trying to win?"

"Well, it could be any number of prizes...a car, an all-expense paid vacation. I'm hoping I'll last until the end for a shot at the cash machine," Ruth said. She went on to explain that the top two finalists literally dashed for cash, around an obstacle course, for a chance to step into a cash box... a Plexiglas booth where wads of cash flew around inside the booth. The final contestant was given a set amount of time to grab as much cash as possible and stuff it into a box inside the booth.

"One of the previous winners posted that the booth was full of tens, twenties and one hundred dollar bills."

"How much were they able to grab?" Gloria asked.

"A cool sixty thousand bucks," Ruth said.

"It must be hard to make it to the cash machine level," Lucy said.

"Difficult, but not impossible, which is why I'll start my training with Kenny again tomorrow morning. It would've been a whole lot easier if I knew what the competitions were going to be. I told him if I get a shot at the cash machine, I'll give him a cut of the winnings."

"That sounds fair," Lucy said. "Is that all there is to the tape?"

"I don't know." Ruth clicked the play button again and the women silently studied the rest of the video, but nothing hit Gloria's sleuthing radar.

She stepped to the side while Ruth unhooked the cable and strapped the watch to her wrist. "We need to take a closer look at the suspects. It's a shame we don't have access to their names so we could do a little more research."

A sly smile crept across Ruth's face. "Oh, but you're wrong. We do."

Chapter 7

"First, I have to log into my work account." Ruth tapped the computer keys and opened a new window. "Now all I need to do..." She turned to Gloria. "Would you like me to email the list or print it off?"

"A print copy please, so I can jot down some notes."

"10-4." Ruth turned her attention to the screen and the printer began to hum. "I also ran off the list of all of the contestants who competed, but were eliminated."

Gloria plucked the sheet of paper off the printer and she studied the list. "How on earth did you get your hands on this list?"

"If I told you, I would have to kill you," Ruth said.

"Meaning we probably don't want to know," Lucy chimed in. "I'm sure Ruth has files on all of us."

"I do not have files on my friends," Ruth said indignantly. "The only reason I have this list is to check out the competition."

"I thought that was what your online chat group was for." Gloria set the sheet of paper on the desk.

"People in those chat groups only tell you what they want you to know. I figured it wouldn't hurt to dig a little deeper, really get the scoop on the others."

Ruth started to push the chair back.

"Oh. Before you go, is there a way to make a copy of the video and audio and send it to me? I may want to go over it again," Gloria said.

"Aye-aye." Ruth lifted her hand in salute. "I'll have to do it from home. I doubt you have the copy capability on your computer. I need to get going. I promised Dot I would stop by the restaurant to tell them what happened today and to thank Rose."

"I need to go, too," Lucy said. "I'm sure Jasper is hungry and ready to go out."

Gloria walked her friends out onto the porch. She promised Ruth she would research the list of contestants and then reminded her to forward a copy of the video when she had time. She waited until both vehicles pulled out of the drive before wandering back inside the house where she found Paul in the living room, watching television.

"Well? Did you solve the mystery?"

"This one might be tricky." Gloria slumped into her recliner and flipped the lever. "I didn't want to say too much in front of Ruth, but it doesn't look good. The fact that Ruth and Amy Mahoney became involved in a physical altercation shortly before her death, not to mention the two exchanged words in the online chat forum doesn't bode well."

She turned her attention to the television and sightlessly stared at the screen. There was one thing that kept playing over and over in Gloria's mind. It was when Amy Mahoney told Ruth she was going down, too. Perhaps if she could figure out whom Amy was referring to besides Ruth, she would be one step closer to figuring out who murdered the woman.

Early the next morning, Gloria whipped up a platter of pancakes and a side of crispy bacon before filling a plastic storage container with the leftover barbecue chicken and placing two hamburger buns in a zip-lock baggie. She placed both inside the cooler, along with a small bag of chips and an apple.

She finished by filling the cooler with bottled waters and then set the cooler in front of the door as Paul stepped into the kitchen and settled into an empty chair.

"Pancakes. My favorite." Paul stabbed a stack of pancakes with his fork and transferred them to his plate before pouring a generous amount of syrup on top. "What's on your agenda today?"

"The first thing on my list is to run by Andrea and Brian's place. Maybe stop by Eleanor's place to see how she's doing. I don't see much of her now that she has her driver's license."

"Or even before she got her driver's license," Paul chuckled. "At least she's legal on the road now."

"Barely." Although Eleanor had passed the required written and road tests, it had taken her two tries to pass the vision exam. Gloria had a sneaking suspicion Eleanor had somehow managed to memorize the lines because she claimed to have passed the second eye test with flying colors.

"That reminds me, Eleanor is still determined to purchase a gun. I keep putting her off, promising her we would run by Lucy's place so she could practice shooting."

"To see if she can hit the broad side of a barn," Paul joked.

"Exactly." Gloria grabbed her cell phone off the table and texted Lucy before setting it back down. "I also plan to stop by Dot's Restaurant to see how Rose is faring after the minor incident at her house the other day."

Paul paused, his fork midair. "Incident? What incident?"

"Oh gosh. I forgot to tell you Rose had a minor mishap with one of her potions the other day and it caught fire. She's fine. Both she and Johnnie are fine. Johnnie put his foot down and is refusing to let her mix her concoctions inside the house. He bought a shed and plans to put it in the backyard for Rose to use."

"I'm surprised no one has called the FDA to report her." Paul finished his last bite of food and reached for his napkin.

"Me too. I mean, her elixirs are harmless, at least from what I can tell, but all it will take is for someone to become ill, or worse, and they somehow trace it back to Rose. What do you think would happen to Rose?"

"I don't know." Paul rinsed his plate in the sink and set that, along with his fork and empty coffee cup inside the dishwasher. "It involves the Feds. Your guess is as good as mine. Of course, if someone is harmed, there's always the sue-happy Logan and Logan law firm in Grand Rapids. They would probably be all over it."

Paul shrugged his jacket on and then wrapped his arms around his wife. "Promise me you'll stay a safe distance from Eleanor if she's shooting guns."

"I'll be sure to be careful." Gloria snuggled close to Paul and placed her head on his chest. "I hope you have a nice day at work."

Paul kissed the top of her head and released his grip. "That's the plan." He grabbed the cooler and strolled out of the house, making his way to the car.

Gloria waved as he pulled out of the driveway and then headed to the bathroom to get ready. Her first stop was Andrea and Brian's place. She'd promised to bring Andrea a batch of pickled cucumbers she'd canned a few weeks earlier after hearing her young friend was craving vinegary foods.

It was exciting to see Andrea happy and in love. She'd been through so much, including the murder of her first husband. And if that in itself wasn't traumatic enough, she made the painful discovery he hadn't been the loving, devoted husband Andrea believed him to be.

Most women would have promptly packed their bags and headed home after going through such an earth-shattering event, but Andrea wasn't most women. She was a fighter and she reminded Gloria of her younger self.

Andrea was also stubborn as a mule. She remembered the day when her young friend announced she was buying the old Johnson place and had plans to restore it. Gloria had been against it, but Andrea proved her...proved everyone wrong when she bought the major fixer-upper and completely renovated it.

Mally sat in front of the door and watched as Gloria slipped her coat on. "Sorry Mally. I don't think I should take you this time since I plan to stop by Lucy's place."

Lucy had replied to Gloria's text, telling her she was catching up on some laundry and would be hanging around home until later in the day.

Gloria patted Mally's head and slipped out onto the porch. A gust of cold wind swirled around the side of the house, and Gloria shivered as she pulled her jacket tighter. Forecasters were predicting a dusting of snow by the weekend, which wasn't out of the ordinary for mid-November.

It was a quick trip to Andrea and Brian's home and Andrea greeted Gloria at the front door, beaming brightly. She looked radiant, and slender...a little too slender in Gloria's opinion. She gave her a quick hug. "You're still too thin."

"You sound like Alice. My appetite is finally starting to come back." She pointed at the Mason jar Gloria was holding. "You remembered the pickles."

"Of course." Gloria handed her the jar. "These pickles aren't going to put meat on your bones and feed that growing baby."

"I promise. I'm eating like a horse. Between Brian and Alice, that's all I'm doing these days."

Brutus trotted down the hall to greet Gloria and she did a double take before bursting out laughing. "What in the world?"

Andrea's pooch was wearing a baby blue crocheted dog cowl around his neck. On one side was a pale pink heart, and she could've sworn the dog was scowling.

"Did you take up crocheting?" Gloria asked.

"Not me," Andrea said. "Brian made it, but don't tell anyone. He's also working on a baby blanket."

"Ah." Gloria remembered the time she and the Garden Girls had been inside Brian's hardware store, searching for clues to try to figure out who had attacked him. During the search, she'd found a stash of knitting needles in one of the drawers. "Brian is a man of many talents."

"You should see the orange pom pom hat he made. Brutus hates that even more than he hates the dog cowl." Andrea motioned Gloria toward the kitchen. "Would you like a cup of coffee? I haven't made any yet. I'm trying to cut down on the caffeine because I don't want to make the baby jittery."

"No thanks. I've had my morning fill." Gloria hopped onto a barstool. "When are you leaving for New York?"

"Next week. Brian finally hired more part-time staff to cover the shifts at the hardware store, the pharmacy and the Quik-Stop. He's finishing up the training this week and then we're off."

"I hope you have a wonderful time visiting with your family."

"Me too. I haven't been back home for a couple of years." Andrea twirled the end of her blonde locks. "Neither has Alice."

"Alice decided to go with you, after all?"

"Yep. It took some convincing. She has a sister who lives in the Bronx, so I think she's going to stay at her house for a couple of days, and then at my parent's place for the rest of the week." Andrea rattled off the list of things she had planned, and although Brian had visited New York on several occasions, the couple had several fun outings they planned to do together while they were there.

"How did Ruth's tryouts for Dash for Cash go?"

"She made the final cut, but one of the other finalists, a woman, was drugged and died from an overdose."

Andrea's hand flew to her mouth. "Drugged? You mean someone killed her?"

"It appears so." Gloria briefly told Andrea what had happened and how the investigators suspected Ruth's involvement because of the confrontation between the two, not to mention the online verbal spats.

"Surely, they can't pin this on Ruth just because of that."

"I think the authorities are leaning in that direction. There were a handful of other contestants inside the maze at the time of the woman's attack. I think it's safe to say we can narrow the list of suspects to that group."

"Let me guess...you're on the case."

"Sort of. Ruth stopped by last night and asked me to take a look at a video she recorded during the second competition."

Andrea shook her head. "Ruth recorded the whole thing?"

"She did, using her spy watch with both audio and video surveillance."

"I've never heard of such a thing. Of course, we're talking about Ruth here."

"Right? What will they think of next?"

The women chatted about the baby, about the fire at the Morris' home and finally, Gloria slid off the stool. "I better get going. I need to stop by Eleanor's place. She's chomping at the bit to buy a handgun. I've been putting her off until Lucy had time to let us stop by her place so Eleanor could practice shooting one of Lucy's guns."

"Gauging Eleanor's skill set," Andrea said. "That sounds like fun."

"Why don't you come with us?"

"I..." Andrea slapped the palm of her hand on the countertop. "I have been cooped up in this house and hovered over for days on end thanks to Brian and Alice. They're both at work now and I could use a little adventure."

Gloria laughed. "Be careful what you wish for. Let's go."

Chapter 8

Eleanor wasn't home, so Gloria and Andrea drove through town, cruising past the Quik-Stop, Dot's Restaurant and the post office before circling the block.

On their second drive by, Andrea spotted Eleanor's car parked in the Church of God parking lot. "I see Eleanor's car."

"You're right. I wonder what she's doing at the church." Gloria pulled into the parking lot and eased into an empty spot. The church's front doors were unlocked, so the women made their way into the lobby where Gloria heard muffled voices coming from the sanctuary. "Hello?"

The echo of heavy footsteps on the tile floor grew louder and Pastor Nate stepped into the lobby. "Uh-oh. A visit from Gloria Kennedy in the middle of the week. Is someone ill?"

"No. Everyone is fine...well, with the exception of a minor dilemma, which involves Ruth. We were actually looking for Eleanor and noticed her car is parked out front."

"She's in the sanctuary. Eleanor has generously offered to play piano during the Sunday morning church services, switching every other week with Sue. Sue and Eleanor are going over everything Eleanor needs to know. They're finishing up."

"That's interesting," Gloria said. "I didn't know Eleanor knew how to play piano." The women followed Pastor Nate down the center aisle, to the front of the sanctuary.

"Hi Gloria." Eleanor, who was seated next to Sue on the piano bench, waved.

"I didn't know you played piano," Andrea said. "Why don't you play something for us?"

Eleanor's face lit up. "Of course. I've been practicing this number for this Sunday's service!" She played a few keys of "happy birthday to you," and Sue tapped her hand and gave a quick shake of her head.

"Oh dear." Eleanor stopped playing. "I did it again, didn't I?"

Sue nodded. "Yes. You're probably just nervous."

"Let me try again." Eleanor poised her fingers over the keys, took a deep breath and began playing and singing, 'How Great Thou Art.'

Gloria closed her eyes and hummed along. They all grew silent, listening to the haunting melody and Eleanor's sweet angelic voice. After the last key faded, Gloria opened her eyes. "That was beautiful, Eleanor."

"Thanks. I've been practicing at home, too, but I'm sure you're not here to listen to my music."

"You're right," Gloria said. "I tried reaching you early this morning. I guess you had already left the house."

"Ruth called me last night, asking if I could meet her at the VFW Hall first thing this morning because she wanted to use some of the free weights before she went into work. Something about a contest."

"Dash for Cash," Andrea and Gloria said in unison. "Ruth is training to be on the game show, Dash for Cash."

"You don't say. I've thought about trying out myself," Eleanor said.

"I'm sure Ruth would be more than happy to give you a few pointers on how to up your odds."

"I wondered why I kept seeing her in sweatpants and a t-shirt, jogging on the sides of the road first thing in the morning," Pastor Nate said. "When will she find out if she makes the cut?"

"She already did, yesterday," Gloria said. "She beat out a bunch of other contestants and made it in the top five."

"I'd love to be there for moral support," Eleanor said. "They're probably taping it out in California or New York. I don't fly."

"You're in luck. Ruth said they'll be taping the show somewhere in Grand Rapids. I'm not sure where yet."

"Oh." Eleanor clasped her hands. "That sounds like fun. I'm in."

"Speaking of fun, I'm here to see if you have time to run by Lucy Carlson's place with us to take a look at her array of arsenal. She's home this morning and said we could stop by."

"What an unusual coincidence," Eleanor said. "I know you promised to take me over to her place, but I was getting antsy to scope out some guns and was planning to run down to All Seasons Sporting Goods this afternoon to take a look around."

"God's timing is perfect."

"It sure is." Eleanor swiveled in a half circle and slid off the piano bench. She grasped the handrail and descended the steps. "Oh Andrea. Congratulations on the baby." She paused. "Are you going to shoot guns, too?"

"No. I'll wait inside while you're practicing," Andrea said. "I was getting a little stir crazy, and Gloria offered to let me tag along with her today."

"I'll text Lucy and let her know we're on our way." Gloria pulled her cell phone from her purse and tapped a message to Lucy. "We don't have to wait for a reply. She said she would be home all morning."

"Before you go." Pastor Nate held up a hand. "Maybe we should pray for safety today."

"Not a bad idea," Gloria mumbled.

Sue joined the circle. They all joined hands and bowed their heads as Pastor Nate began to pray. "Dear Heavenly Father. Thank you for all of your many blessings in our lives. We pray for Andrea and Brian, and the new life Andrea is carrying.

Lord, we give this little one to you and ask that he continues to thrive, he's perfectly formed, so when he or she greets us on that much-anticipated day, all of these wonderful Belhaven grandmas can spoil him, love him and cherish him, as his or her parents will do."

The pastor continued. "Lord, we also pray for safety today, as Gloria, Andrea and Eleanor make their way to Lucy's place to practice shooting guns."

"And keep Eleanor's aim straight," Gloria quipped.

"Amen." Pastor Nate said.

"Amen," the women echoed.

"Thank you Pastor Nate," Gloria said. "Now let's go shoot some guns."

Eleanor followed Gloria and Andrea back through town and toward Lucy's place.

Gloria pulled in the drive first and Eleanor parked behind her.

Lucy emerged from her shed and met them in the drive. "Andrea. Oh, it's good to see you venturing out." She gave her a warm hug. "You aren't here to shoot guns, are you?"

"No," Andrea shook her head. "I'm going to hang out in the house during the shooting part."

Lucy waited until Eleanor was out of the car to greet her. "Oh Eleanor. Look at you. All gussied up in your Sunday best, just to shoot guns."

"I had a meeting at the church," Eleanor said. "I'm going to start playing piano during the Sunday morning services, starting this Sunday. Sue and I will be taking turns every other week."

"I didn't know you knew how to play piano."

"It's been awhile. I'm a little rusty, but both Sue and Pastor Nate said I was good enough to play at the gates of heaven."

"She most certainly is." Gloria patted Eleanor's arm.

"I can't wait to hear you this Sunday." Lucy linked arms with Eleanor, and they strolled toward the shed. "I wasn't sure if you had already eaten breakfast, so I have some fresh coffee and pastries in the shed."

Lucy turned to Andrea. "I had no idea you were coming, but I even picked up a couple of blueberry muffins...your favorite."

"Thanks Lucy. Blueberry muffins sound delish."

Lucy led them to the workbench in the center of the shed where there was a carafe of coffee, several coffee cups and a small stack of disposable plates. Gloria peered into the boxes of donuts. "You bought all of these for us?"

"Well, maybe not all. The doctor said I'm doing such a stellar job of lowering my cholesterol, I can indulge in a sweet or two every once in a while."

As the women munched on their treats and sipped their coffee, Gloria told Eleanor all that had transpired during the Dash for Cash competition, about Amy Mahoney's attack inside the maze and how the authorities were questioning Ruth about her death.

"Oh no," Eleanor said. "Ruth wouldn't hurt a fly. It must've been an inside job."

"Yeah, as in – inside-the-maze job," Gloria said. "The woman, Amy Mahoney, made an odd comment to Ruth right before the maze competition started."

"Oh? What kind of comment?" Andrea asked.

"Something along the lines of 'you're both going down,' whatever that means," Gloria said. "Ruth videotaped both the maze competition as well as the tag elimination competition. My plan is to study the tape."

"Don't forget about the list of contestants Ruth gave you," Lucy reminded her.

"Right. Ruth also managed to get her hands on a copy of the contestant list and she gave me a copy."

After they finished eating, Gloria carried the empty coffee cups and leftover goodies to the house while Lucy pointed out several of the weapons, explaining each to Eleanor. She even offered suggestions on the ones she thought might be a good fit for the woman. "I would go with something lightweight and compact that you can carry in your purse."

Gloria, who had returned from taking care of the dishes, interrupted. "Not that Lucy is telling you it's a good idea to carry a gun around in your purse."

Eleanor frowned. "I don't plan on carrying it around. I want to keep one at my house in case someone tries to break in and rob me. Remember that psycho, Lynda Clemson? I need a new weapon since I've retired my walker."

After examining several of the weapons, Eleanor selected a gun to try and then Lucy showed her how to load it. Eleanor practiced loading and unloading the gun until Lucy was satisfied she had it down pat.

"I'll head inside now," Andrea said. "Good luck."

Lucy handed Eleanor and Gloria a set of goggles and earmuffs. "Safety first. We all need to wear earmuffs and goggles. Follow me." They followed Lucy along the sidewalk until they stood roughly ten yards away from a large piece of plywood. Taped to the front was the silhouette of a figure. Inside the figure were several rings, marked with numbers. "This is the target. The goal is to strike the 'x' in the middle."

"I'll demonstrate," Lucy said. "You need to stand at least ten feet behind me."

Gloria and Eleanor backed up. Lucy shifted her stance and raised her gun to eye level before adjusting her earmuffs and steadying her hand. She fired off several rounds, nearly nailing the 'x' every time.

"Impressive," Gloria complimented. "I'll be lucky if I hit the target."

Lucy handed her gun to Gloria. "Let's see whatcha got."

Gloria traded places with Lucy and, following Lucy's lead, adjusted her stance before leveling the weapon. She closed one eye and pulled the trigger.

After firing the gun, Gloria lowered the weapon, inspected the target and held out the gun. "Hey! I hit it."

"You sure did. That's it?" Lucy asked.

"Yeah. I don't want to press my luck. First time was the charm."

It was finally Eleanor's turn.

"Well? Are you ready to give it a shot?"

"As ready as I'll ever be."

Just to be safe, Gloria took several steps back as Lucy coached Eleanor on her aim, her stance and the position of the gun. "Stay steady. Even if you miss, don't worry, there's nothing you could possibly hurt."

"Okay." Eleanor nodded. "I think I'm ready."

Lucy took a step back and gave Eleanor an encouraging nod.

Gloria clasped her hands and tucked them under her chin as Eleanor abruptly swung to the left and fired off a shot, hitting the corner of Lucy's outbuilding. *Bap.*

Bap. The second shot hit the ground and a spray of dirt flew into the air.

Gloria dove for cover.

"Eleanor stop! Lucy lunged for the gun, wrestling it from Eleanor's grip.

"What..." Eleanor frowned. "How did I do?"

"Perfect if your goal was to blow off a chunk of my shingles and stir up a dirt storm." She pointed to the corner of her outbuilding. "You blew a hole clean through it."

"I...where was I supposed to shoot?" Eleanor squinted her eyes and Gloria marched forward. "Eleanor, where are your glasses?"

"They're at home. My vision has been improving lately, so I figured I would try a day without them. It's not like I needed them to play the piano at church."

Gloria pressed her hands to her cheeks. "You should try going without your glasses when you'll be home all day...say...sweeping the floor or cleaning your toilets, but not when you get behind the wheel of a car."

"Or practice shooting a gun," Lucy added.

"Well, I didn't know I was going to be shooting guns when I left the house this morning," Eleanor said in a small voice. She turned to Lucy. "I'm sorry about your roof. I'll pay to have your shingles replaced."

"It's okay Eleanor," Lucy said. "I'm glad no one got hurt."

The women silently trudged back to the shed.

"Thanks for trying to teach me how to shoot Lucy." Eleanor handed the goggles and earmuffs to her friend. "I think I'm going to hold off on purchasing a gun and give it more thought."

"And perhaps practice again, but this time with your glasses on," Gloria added.

Lucy returned the weapons to their proper places and then waited for Eleanor and Gloria to exit the building before locking the doors. "How's Ruth?"

"I don't know. I was going to stop by the post office a little later," Gloria said.

"Are you done already?" Andrea waddled down the steps.

"Yeah. I think we've done enough damage to Lucy's place for the day," Gloria said.

The women chatted a few more moments before thanking Lucy again.

Gloria slid into the driver's seat and noticed her cell phone, which was sitting in the center console, was beeping.

She flipped it over and studied the screen. It was the Belhaven post office. "Speaking of the devil." She pressed the talk button and held the phone to her ear. "Hi Ruth. Were your ears burning?"

"Hey Gloria. Kenny here. I was hoping Ruth was with you."

"No. Isn't Ruth working?"

"She left here a while ago, during her break and told me she'd be right back, but she never returned. I've been trying to reach her for a couple of hours now on her cell phone. I also tried calling her house...she isn't answering."

Chapter 9

"Did she mention where she was going?" Gloria asked.

"No. She was acting a little off all morning, and secretive, too. She kept her cell phone with her and wouldn't stop fiddling with it. When her break time rolled around, she said she needed to run a quick errand and would be right back."

"Did she walk or drive?" Visions of Ruth, lying in an alley unconscious, crept into Gloria's head.

"She took her van, but Ruth couldn't have gone too far because she said she'd be back in a few minutes. I would have gone looking for her, but if I close the post office, we'll both be in trouble."

"I'm here with Lucy and Eleanor. We'll hop in our cars and start searching for her," Gloria said. "Hang tight. We'll call you as soon as we know something or better yet, we'll send Ruth back to the post office."

"Thanks Gloria. I'm already late in starting my morning route."

Gloria promised they would start searching immediately, told Kenny good-bye, and then disconnected the call. "Ruth left the post office during her break this morning, telling Kenny she had a quick errand to run and she hasn't come back yet. Kenny tried calling her cell phone and home phone, but she isn't answering."

"Oh no," Eleanor said. "I hope she's all right."

"Me too." Gloria turned to Lucy. "I know you planned to head out to the flip project. If you have a few extra minutes to spare, maybe you can help us search for her."

"Of course. Friends come first," Lucy said. "In fact, let me give Margaret a quick call to see if she can help search, too." She darted into her house and returned with her cell phone moments later.

"Margaret is on her way. We need to come up with a plan to cover more ground."

While the women waited for Margaret to arrive, they mapped out a search area, planning to spread out across Belhaven and Montbay County. Eleanor offered to search the Lake Terrace neighborhood. Lucy would swing by the flea market and the east side of town while Gloria planned to run by Ruth's house.

The women paused when they heard the screech of tires and Margaret roared into the driveway. She slammed on the brakes and bolted from her car. "Any news on Ruth?"

"Not yet," Gloria said. She briefly outlined the search parameters.

Margaret nodded. "Sounds good. I'll stop by Dot's Restaurant first. If I don't get a hit, I'll head to the Quik-Stop and work my way down Main Street."

"Should we call Officer Joe to give him a heads up?" Lucy asked.

"It's too early to file a missing person's report, but it certainly wouldn't hurt to ask him to be on the lookout for Ruth, too, since he travels all over the county," Gloria said. "I'll give him a call on my way to Ruth's place."

"I'll ride with Margaret," Andrea offered. "We can cover the stores and businesses more quickly if we ride together and then split up."

"Times a wastin'," Eleanor said.

The women sprang into action, each piling into their vehicle and heading out to search for Ruth. Eleanor and Lucy headed to the other side of town while Margaret, along with Andrea, parked in front of Dot's Restaurant.

Gloria continued on, past the post office. A fleeting thought that Ruth had become depressed over the recent turn of events and the police questioning her, ran through her head.

She tightened her grip on the steering wheel as she drove through town and turned onto Ruth's street. The driveway was empty and Gloria started to drive past, but made a last minute decision to pull in and check the house, just to be sure.

She climbed out of her car and made her way to the back porch. Gloria rang the bell and peered through the window, into the small breezeway leading into the kitchen.

There was no sign of movement and Ruth didn't answer, so Gloria stepped off the porch and headed to the front door. Again, Gloria rang the bell and waited. There was no answer, so she circled around the side and strode to Ruth's one-stall detached garage.

Gloria passed by the garage door, walked to the small side door and grasped the knob. The door swung open and Gloria's heart skipped a beat when she spotted Ruth's van, parked inside.

"Oh no." Gloria slammed the door shut and ran back to the porch door where she began pounding on it. "Ruth! It's me, Gloria! Ruth, are you in there?"

Gloria began rattling the knob, willing the door to open and finally gave up before racing to the front door, where she pounded loudly, all the while yelling Ruth's name.

The palms of her hands started to sting. "I need someone who can pick the lock."

She jogged back to her car to grab her cell phone. Gloria's hand trembled as she scrolled the list of contacts, searching for Lucy's number.

Thankfully, Lucy answered on the first ring. "Did you find her?"

"I don't know. I'm here at her house. Ruth's van is parked in the garage, but all of the house doors are locked and she's not answering. Can you come over here and pick the lock? We need to get inside."

Lucy promised she was en route and Gloria made her way back to the porch to peek inside, all the while praying she wouldn't find an unconscious...or worse...dead friend inside.

Gloria shaded her eyes and pressed her forehead against the windowpane. Nothing appeared to be out of place.

She moved to the next window, Ruth's spare bedroom, where Ruth kept her collection of spy gadgets and gizmos. The curtains were closed and Gloria couldn't see inside.

She rounded the corner, where the bathroom was located, but without a ladder, the window was too high to see inside, so she continued on to the master bedroom window. Gloria bounced up on the tips of her toes, trying to peer through the slats of the vertical blinds.

A wave of pure horror engulfed Gloria when she spotted Ruth slumped against the doorway, her eyes closed.

Gloria frantically rapped on the windowpane, but Ruth remained motionless. She snatched her cell phone from her pocket and dialed 911. "Yes, this is Gloria Kennedy. I need an ambulance at 122 Peach Tree Street in Belhaven. My friend,

Ruth Carpenter, is unconscious. Her doors are locked and I'm unable to get to her."

The 911 operator repeated the address and told Gloria she had dispatched an ambulance, as well as a nearby patrol car.

Gloria disconnected the line after thanking the dispatcher. She shoved her cell phone in her pocket and tugged hard on the windowpane. It refused to budge. Her eyes darted around the yard as she began searching for an object to break the window when she caught a glimpse of Lucy's yellow jeep fly into the drive.

"Thank God." Gloria ran to Lucy's jeep. "I found Ruth! She's in the doorway of her bedroom. I pounded on the window and yelled, but she's not responding. An ambulance is on the way. I was thinking that maybe you could try to pick the lock while we wait. Our only other option is to bust out one of her windows."

"Let me try picking the lock first." Lucy grabbed a small case from the console and the women raced to the porch door.

Lucy dropped to her knees and snagged one of the slender tools from the case. "Shoot! Ruth has one of those expensive door locks that are hard to pick. Not impossible, though."

She jabbed the end of the tool into the keyhole, desperately twisting it back and forth. "This one is too small."

Lucy pulled out another tool, this one a little thicker and repeated the steps as she jabbed it inside the keyhole.

Click. "I think I got it." Lucy twisted the knob and the door swung open. She scrambled to her feet and she, along with Gloria, darted into the kitchen, through the dining room to Ruth's bedroom where they found their friend lying in the doorway.

The women dropped to their knees and Gloria touched Ruth's arm. "Ruth. Can you hear me?"

She gently nudged her friend's arm and Ruth's eyes started to flutter.

"Gluria," Ruth slurred her words. "What are you dooo-int?"

"Ruth." Gloria said the first thing that popped into her head. "An ambulance is on the way. Did you take something?"

Confused, Ruth shook her head. "What?"

"Are you still taking Rose's potion?"

"Lemme f...ink." Ruth closed her eyes.

"Ruth, stay with us," Gloria said. "Help is on the way."

The faint sound of sirens filled the air and Gloria was never happier to hear them.

Lucy sprang to her feet. "I'll let them in."

She returned less than a minute later, accompanied by paramedics and Officer Nelson.

Gloria crawled out of the way and watched in horror as the paramedics worked on Ruth. She was still incoherent and had difficulty answering the EMTs questions.

"I'll get the stretcher," the second EMT said.

"I'll help." Officer Nelson followed the EMT out of the bedroom.

Gloria joined Lucy, and they clasped hands as they watched the men ease Ruth onto the stretcher. They secured her legs and chest and then carefully wheeled the stretcher to the porch door before lifting it up and carrying it to the back of the ambulance.

"Which one of you found Ruth?" Officer Nelson asked.

"I did," Gloria said. "When I got here, I noticed Ruth's van was parked in the garage. She didn't answer the door, so I started making my way to each of the windows, searching for signs of her. That's when I saw her slumped in the bedroom doorway."

"Gloria called me to come over and I picked the lock. Ruth's words were slurred and she seemed to be fading in and out consciousness."

The ambulance pulled onto the street, sirens blaring and lights flashing. "I need to head to the hospital to be with Ruth."

"I'll run by the post office to let Kenny know what's going on." Lucy said. "I'll call the others to let them know we found Ruth and then meet you at the hospital."

Officer Nelson reached out to stop them. "I know you're concerned for Ruth's welfare. She's in good hands now. Be careful on the roads. It's hard to focus when you're distraught, and the last thing Ruth needs right now is for one of you to get in an automobile accident."

Gloria's lower lip started to tremble and she nodded. "I'll drive safely."

Officer Joe gave the women a sympathetic smile before returning to his police cruiser and driving off.

"Let's pray." Lucy and Gloria joined hands.

"Dear Heavenly Father," Gloria whispered. "We come to you with heavy hearts, Lord. We know you're Jehovah Rapha, the God who heals, and we need you to touch Ruth. Something is wrong with Ruth, terribly wrong. Please be with the doctors, let them figure out what is going on." Overcome with emotion, Gloria broke down and began sobbing.

"Please be with her Lord," Lucy added and then burst into tears.

Gloria reached across Ruth's counter, tore off a couple of paper towels and handed one to Lucy. "We're not doing Ruth any good standing here bawling our eyes out."

"I need to round up the others." Lucy blew her nose and then tossed the paper towel in the garbage can. "Be careful going to the hospital and we'll all be careful meeting you there. In the meantime, if you hear anything, anything at all, please call me."

"I will," Gloria promised. She followed Lucy out of the house before locking the door and pulling it shut. "We have to believe Ruth will be all right. She has to be."

Gloria climbed into her car and drove toward the Green Springs Memorial Hospital. During the ride, she pleaded with God, argued with him, laid out all of the reasons Ruth needed to make a complete recovery.

When she reached the emergency entrance parking lot, she shut the car off, bowed her head and prayed for something that had eluded her from the moment she spotted Ruth on the floor...peace. Gloria prayed for peace.

When she lifted her head, she sucked in a breath and pushed the car door open. Ruth was going to be all right, Ruth had to be all right.

Chapter 10

With deliberate, measured steps, Gloria walked to the emergency room reception desk. "Yes, my name is Gloria Kennedy. My friend, Ruth Carpenter, was brought here by ambulance."

Gloria's voice began to crack, and she paused as she fought to keep her emotions in check. "I'm...the closest thing to family Ruth has. Could you please tell me if I'm in the right area and where they may have taken her?"

A flash of sympathy crossed the receptionist's face, and she turned her attention to the computer screen. "Can you spell her name?"

"It's R-U-T-H C-A-R-P-E-N-T-E-R."

The woman tapped her keyboard, a frown crossing her face. "I don't see a record of her admittance yet. The EMT's call would have been dispatched to the emergency room nurse's station. It's possible they took her directly to one of the ER examination areas. If you have some of her basic information, I can enter it in the computer."

Gloria rattled off Ruth's address and date of birth, Ruth's sister's name as next of kin, but told the receptionist her sister lived in Florida. She was still at the front desk, attempting to provide the receptionist with Ruth's information when Lucy, Margaret, Eleanor, Dot, Rose and Andrea rushed in.

They waited patiently for her to finish speaking to the receptionist, and after giving what information she could, Gloria joined her friends.

"How's Ruth?" Lucy asked.

"I don't know yet. The front desk had no record of Ruth, and the receptionist said they probably took her right to the back for treatment."

"Oh my goodness," Rose fretted. "This is terrible. I spoke with Ruth this morning. She said she was feeling a little lightheaded. I figured it was a carryover from the stress of the contests, not to mention being questioned by the police in the other contestant's death."

"I need to call Kenny," Gloria said. "Maybe he can fill in some blanks, too. Perhaps Ruth complained of other symptoms that might be useful to the doctors." She dialed the post office number, and it rang several times before a breathless Kenny picked up. "Belhaven Post Office. Kenny Webber speaking."

"Kenny, it's Gloria. I'm at the hospital waiting for an update on Ruth's condition. Rose said she complained that she was feeling lightheaded this morning. Is there anything you can recall Ruth saying?"

"Now that you mention it, she said she skipped breakfast and was feeling lightheaded and tired. She was also having trouble reading the mail. I thought it had something to do with her being distracted by her cell phone. Maybe it was something else."

"Is that all?"

"Yeah. I hope she's going to be okay. I'm worried sick. The post office is a madhouse. Everyone has been in here, asking about Ruth after several people spotted the ambulance at her house. Hang on."

Gloria listened to Kenny's muffled reply to someone.

"I'll let you go, Kenny. Thanks for the information. I'll pass it on to the doctor."

"Call me as soon as you have word," Kenny said.

"I promise, I will." Gloria thanked Kenny again and disconnected the call. "He said she was complaining of feeling fatigued and lightheaded, and had skipped breakfast."

Gloria returned to the receptionist's desk to tell the woman what she'd learned and then joined her friends. "She said we should hear something soon."

The group assembled off in the corner, to a cluster of chairs where they could all sit together. While they waited, Gloria and Lucy repeated the events of the morning, when Kenny called, and how Gloria panicked when she spotted Ruth unconscious and in her bedroom doorway. "I almost broke the window, but then I had the idea to call Lucy. She picked the lock on Ruth's back door."

"You picked the lock?" Eleanor gasped.

"It's a little uh...talent I have," Lucy said.

"Picking locks, shooting guns, hunting wild animals" Eleanor said. "You were born in the wrong era."

"She should've been born in the Wild, Wild West back in the 1800's," Margaret joked.

Lucy frowned. "No way would you get me into a petticoat, hoopskirt or any of that jazz."

Visions of Lucy squeezed into a frilly dress with layers of ruffles caused Gloria to grin. "Now I would like to see that."

A man in a white medical jacket strode into the area. He spoke briefly with the receptionist before crossing the room and approaching the group. "Are you here with Ruth Carpenter?"

"We are." Gloria stood. "Ruth's niece is in Grand Rapids, and her sister lives in Florida. We're the closest thing to family. Is there news on Ruth's condition?"

"I'm Doctor Stone, the emergency room physician who was on duty when Ruth arrived," he said. "Ruth is going to be okay."

"Thank God," Dot pressed a hand against her chest. "What happened?"

"We're still running a few tests, but it appears Ruth experienced a dip in her blood sugar."

Andrea frowned. "Is Ruth diabetic?"

"We're not sure yet. Ruth told me she's never been diagnosed with diabetes." The doctor continued. "The fact she skipped breakfast, exercised early, before work and was taking some sort of..."

"Herbal energy supplement," Margaret suggested, her eyes sliding to Rose.

"Yes." Dr. Stone shoved his hands in his pockets. "From the sounds of it, she may want to take a closer look at the supplement's ingredients."

Rose opened her mouth and promptly shut it.

We're stabilizing her blood sugar now, and she should be ready to go home later this evening. If you'd like to see her, I can take you to her room."

The women all scrambled to their feet. "Yes. Please."

Dr. Stone's long strides covered the room in record time, and the women had to pick up the pace to keep up with him.

They passed the reception area, turned left, and he led them through a set of double doors, past a nurse's station.

"This looks familiar," Dot hissed.

"This is where they brought Brian after he was attacked at his hardware store and suffered from amnesia," Andrea reminded her.

"That's right," Margaret said. "This is also where we were first introduced to Rose's potions."

"Which cured Brian of his amnesia," Rose pointed out.

The doctor abruptly stopped in front of an open door. "Ruth is in here."

The women tiptoed into the room; Gloria paused before entering the room as she thanked the doctor for taking care of Ruth.

He smiled. "She's got a stubborn streak, I'll give you that. We'll be lucky if she'll stay put long enough for us to finish running our tests and processing her release papers."

"Sounds about right." Gloria followed her friends to the other side of the room where she found Ruth sitting in the bedside chair, pulling on her shoes. "What are you doing?"

"Blowing this popsicle stand," Ruth said. "I feel fine. So I needed to eat some food, I got a little dizzy and hit the floor."

"You scared us half to death," Gloria scolded. "The doctor said he's running some tests to determine if you're diabetic."

"I doubt it," Ruth reached for her other sock. "I'm strong as a horse, never sick a day in my life, except for the time Bea McQueen gave me the flu."

"There's a first time for everything," Dot calmly replied. "Your health is very important, and you need to look at this as a wakeup call."

Dot's words began to sink in. Ruth set her shoe in her lap, her eyes circling the room as she studied the somber faces surrounding her.

"I'm sorry," Ruth said. "I didn't mean to scare you. You're right, Dot. I do need to take better care of myself. I've been putting off my yearly checkup for two years now, not to mention my mammogram."

Gloria glanced at Dot, noting the pinched expression on her face.

"You need to go in for checkups. I'll go with you if you don't want to go alone," Dot quietly said.

Tears welled up in Gloria's eyes and she blinked rapidly. "Perfect. We're going to hold your feet to the fire on this one, Ruth."

"I'm sure you will," Ruth sighed.

A nurse slipped into the room, pushing a cart. "We need to check a few more things Ms. Carpenter."

"We'll wait in the hall," Andrea said.

The women exited the room single file and huddled in the hall. "I wasn't kidding about holding Ruth's feet to the fire," Gloria said. "If we don't keep on her, she won't go."

"We will," Eleanor said. "Our health is one of the most important things we have."

"I couldn't agree more, Eleanor."

Dot glanced at her watch. "I need to get back to the restaurant. Rose and I ran out of the restaurant so fast, Johnnie and Ray were busting their butts trying to keep up."

"Go on," Gloria said. "I'll stay behind until they release Ruth."

"I'll stay with you," Lucy offered.

"Me too," Margaret said.

"I'll ride back with Dot," Andrea said.

"You can ride home with me, Andrea," Eleanor said. "Your house is on my way home."

Andrea's eyes widened and she placed a protective hand on her baby bump. "I..."

"I'll drive slowly and cautiously," Eleanor promised.

"Without your glasses?" Gloria reminded her.

"Fine. I'll let Andrea drive my car," Eleanor said.

Gloria promised her friends she would let them know if there was any change in Ruth's diagnosis or release and then waited for them to exit the emergency room area before Margaret, Lucy, and she returned to Ruth's side.

Ruth had already removed her socks and was back in bed.

"Good girl," Gloria said.

"I'm not in here by choice," Ruth grumbled. "That nurse is one tough cookie. She told me I had to get back in bed or else she wasn't going to authorize my release until tomorrow."

"You've met your match," Margaret said.

Ruth smoothed the bedsheet. "How did you find me?"

"Kenny called to ask if I'd seen you. He told me you went on break and never returned and he was worried," Gloria said. "Of course, he couldn't leave work. He asked if we could try to track you down. Luckily, Eleanor, Andrea and I were at Lucy's place, shooting guns."

Ruth interrupted. "You gave Eleanor a weapon?"

"Under direct supervision," Lucy said.

"After we finished shooting, we were heading back to our cars when Kenny called. He'd been trying to reach you for a couple of hours. We knew something was wrong. I called Margaret to come by, so that we could all search and cover more ground quickly."

Gloria went on to tell Ruth how at first, she thought she wasn't home, but then spotted her van in the garage and decided to take a closer look. "That's when I saw you in your bedroom doorway."

"How did you get into my house? I know I locked the porch door when I got home."

"I picked the lock," Lucy said.

"You picked my lock? Impossible. I installed one of those European multi-point door locks. It was supposed to be virtually pick proof."

"You might want to get your money back because Lucy had that baby open in less than ten seconds," Gloria said.

"What a rip off." Ruth frowned. "Not only were they more expensive, those stupid locks took forever to install."

"Remind me to change the locks on my doors," Margaret teased.

"I wouldn't pick anyone's lock unless it was an emergency, like we had today with Ruth," Lucy argued. "It's not like I have loads of free time to run around picking people's locks."

"You did the right thing, Lucy." Gloria changed the subject. "I haven't had a chance to look at the contestant list you gave me."

"I started to try to match the online chat members to the contestants," Ruth said. "I sent you the link to log onto the chat group. While I was in there last night, I found out something very interesting about Amy Mahoney, the contestant who died."

Chapter 11

"Amy Mahoney was the niece of Gerald Marsh, the show's production manager," Ruth said. "He's in charge of the show's scheduling and making sure the production runs smoothly."

She went on to explain how one of the other posters suggested the only way Mahoney made it to the elimination rounds was because of her connections. "And then someone else chimed in, someone I've never heard of before. She said half the finalists for Dash for Cash had connections."

"It doesn't seem fair," Lucy said.

"I agree and I need to do some more research, but until the hospital releases me, I'm dead in the water lying in this bed," Ruth said. "While I was waiting, I've been mentally going over the list of suspects, the other finalists inside the maze."

"Hang on." Gloria held up a hand. "Let me get a notepad and pen out of my purse." She pulled out the items and flipped the top of the small notepad. "Fire away."

"First, there's Desiree Warner. I think she's a fitness instructor and if I remember correctly, a former corrections officer."

"Got it." Gloria scribbled the name and jotted notes next to it.

"Then there's Lane Jorgensen. Male. From the east side of the state and I don't know much about him. He's young. After that, there's Ivy Barnett. Now that I think about Ivy, she may be the online user with the name *dashboard*. I think Ivy has been a contestant before."

Gloria wrote Ivy's name with a dash next to it and then the name *dashboard*. "This is really going to help."

"And, of course, Mahoney and me," Ruth said.

"Margaret and I can hang around and one of us will drive Ruth home later," Lucy said. "There's no sense in all of us sitting here now that we know Ruth is going to be okay."

"You have a point." Gloria glanced at the clock on the wall. "If I head home now, I'll have plenty of time to take a closer look at the list of contestants and do a little digging around."

"That would be great," Ruth beamed. "Maybe we can start piecing this mystery together and Detective Rat Breath will leave me alone."

Gloria snorted. "Detective Rat Breath?"

"The detective who's in charge of investigating Mahoney's death. He talks like this." Ruth began to enunciate her words, exaggerating each syllable. "He's a greasy fellow, for lack of a better word and his breath smells like a decaying rat."

"Gross," Margaret wrinkled her nose. "He must have at least one redeeming quality."

"Yeah...he didn't arrest me."

Gloria rolled her eyes as she leaned over the side of the bed. "I'm glad to see you're okay. You're not allowed to scare us like that ever again."

"I won't." Ruth smiled softly. "Thanks for caring enough about me to break into my house and rescue me."

"You're welcome. I love you, my friend." Once again, tears threatened, and Gloria blinked them back as she gently hugged Ruth. "Life wouldn't be the same without you. I'll start on the investigation as soon as I get home."

Lucy and Margaret promised to call Gloria when Ruth was released, and then Gloria slowly made her way out of the hospital and to her car, thanking God for sparing Ruth and for putting her and the other friends in the right place at the right time.

***

Gloria swung by a fast food restaurant on her way home, grabbing a cheeseburger and a small order of French fries. It had been hours since she'd eaten and she was beginning to feel sick to her stomach.

When she reached the house, she let Mally out for a run and then headed back inside to the computer. She logged onto her email and quickly located Ruth's messages. One was a note, giving Gloria her login information for the Dash for Cash chat group.

Curious to read the comments Ruth had mentioned, Gloria decided to start there and began scrolling through the comments. She found the one from another poster who mentioned Amy Mahoney's relationship to the show's production manager, Gerald Marsh.

She clicked on the user name *dashboard*, but it was only a silhouette with vague information. Gloria clicked through a few more of the user's comments and her investigative radar hit high gear. *Dashboard* appeared to know an awful lot about the inner workings of the game show.

Gloria rifled through her top file bin and pulled out the list of contestants Ruth had printed the previous night. She grabbed a pen and wrote Dash for Cash suspects at the top of the sheet. Next to Ivy Barnett's name, she wrote *dashboard* with a question mark.

Gloria turned her attention to some of the older comments. Most were posts from other contestants, shocked Mahoney had died during the competition, and several hinting perhaps a fellow contestant was responsible for Mahoney's death, a reasonable assumption considering there was both motive and opportunity.

She studied the list and attempted to match the names to the online user names, but it was useless. She had no clue who the people were.

Gloria tapped her pen on top of the paper and mulled over Ruth's revelation that Amy Mahoney was related to Gerald Marsh.

Another online user suggested there might be other contestants who were related to the Dash for Cash staff. A thought popped into Gloria's head, and she opened a new search screen, typed "cast and crew of the Dash for Cash game show" and began scrolling through the list.

The first two were dead ends. When she opened the third site, she hit pay dirt...a list of the current staff, including the executive producer, the associate producer, the consulting producer and a long list of others. "How many people does it take to create a half hour game show?" Gloria muttered under her breath.

She compared the list of staff members with the list Ruth had given her of all of the original contestants when she stumbled upon a match. Travis Baexter shared the same last name as Michael Baexter, the show's assistant to the executive producer. There was a possibility it was a coincidence, but then again, the spelling of their last names was unusual.

Gloria carefully jotted Michael Baexter and assistant to the executive producer next to Travis' name.

She continued her search, but none of the other contestant names appeared to be linked to the show's staff.

A tiny stabbing pain in Gloria's temple threatened to turn into a bigger headache, so she logged off the internet and slid out of the chair.

Puddles wandered into the dining room and began circling Gloria's legs. She scooped him up and held him close. "Where have you been hiding? You're usually on my lap before I even have a chance to fire up the computer."

In response, Puddles began to purr and butted Gloria's chin with his head. She carried him to the kitchen and gently set him on the floor before reaching into the pantry and pulling out a tin of his favorite kitty treats.

She shook some into the palm of her hand and then held them out while Puddles munched on the treats.

Mally, who was watching them from her doggie bed, let out a low whine.

"Of course I can't forget you." She replaced the lid on the treats and grabbed Mally's box of treats, placing a small heap of crunchy snacks on the linoleum floor. "Now what to do about dinner?"

Gloria made her way to the pantry, opened the door and peered inside at the meager supply of staples. "I guess it's time for a trip to the grocery store."

She grabbed her yellow pad and began working on a grocery list. After finishing the list, Mally and she headed to the porch. The air was cool, but the sun was shining and it gave off enough warmth to warrant a few stolen moments in the rocker.

Gloria eased into the chair and stared at the small farm across the road. She thought of Ruth's scare and of Don's death earlier in the year. Then she thought about Dot's recent biopsy. She closed her eyes and leaned her head back.

What if Dot's cancer had returned? Would Ray and she finally retire and sell the restaurant? Would Johnnie and Rose stay on? They were questions Gloria was sure kept Ray and Dot up at night. *Lord, Please give Dot negative results for her biopsy,* she pleaded and prayed. *Thank you for Ruth's recovery. Thank you for all of our blessings.*

Gloria lifted her head, eased out of the rocker and stepped back inside the house. She still had no idea what to fix for dinner, so she texted Paul to ask if he minded eating Dinner at Dot's.

It took several minutes for him to reply, and he told his wife that was fine with him. She didn't bother telling him all that had transpired or about Ruth's scare. It would take too long, and there would be plenty of time to discuss it later.

As if on cue, Gloria received a second text, this one from Margaret, letting her know they were with Ruth, on the way home from the hospital and Ruth was craving Dot's chicken 'n dumplings, so they planned to swing by for dinner.

"I'll meet you there," Gloria texted back, then sent Paul a reply, telling him she'd meet him at Dot's, as well.

Gloria beat her friends to the restaurant and then made her way to an empty table, large enough to seat everyone including Dot and Rose.

Dot was nowhere in sight. Rose spotted Gloria first. She made her way over and set a glass of ice water on the table. "Is there any news on Ruth?"

"Yes. Margaret, Lucy and Ruth are on their way here. Ruth is craving Dot's dumplings. I was already planning to have dinner here with Paul, so we all decided to meet."

"Thank goodness. I'm glad to hear Ruth is okay." Rose rubbed the tip of her nose. "I feel somewhat responsible for her incident, what with her taking my potion and not eating."

Gloria patted Rose's arm. "Don't blame yourself. Ruth is an adult. It was a series of unfortunate events. The important thing is she's okay."

"I appreciate your words of encouragement. Between me setting fire to the house and Ruth's collapse, I've made one too many visits to the hospital lately. Maybe it's time for me to pack in the potions."

"I think you should think about it." Gloria shifted in her seat. "Take Eleanor, for example. You've given the woman a new lease on life. I'm not going to tell you what to do one way or the other. This has to be your decision. All I'm suggesting is that you think about it."

"I will," Rose promised. She left a stack of menus on the table before heading to the kitchen.

Dot passed her on the way. She pulled out a chair and plopped down next to Gloria. "I heard Ruth is on her way here."

"She's craving your chicken 'n dumplings," Gloria said. "How are you feeling Dot? Have you heard back from the doctor?"

"Yes," Dot said. "It was so crazy around here earlier; I didn't have time to tell you the results came back. They were negative."

"Thank God." Gloria closed her eyes briefly. "I've been praying."

"I know you have and I love you for it." Dot gave a quick glance toward the kitchen. "Did Rose tell you she's thinking about shuttering her new side business...the sale of her special elixir mixtures?"

"Yeah. She feels responsible for Ruth's incident, not to mention the fire at her home. I told her to think about it."

"I did too. Have you had a chance to start researching the Dash for Cash contestants?"

"I did," Gloria nodded. "In fact, I found out a couple of very interesting things."

There was a loud commotion near the door and Gloria stopped talking to watch Ruth, Margaret and Lucy enter the restaurant. Several well-wishers surrounded Ruth.

Finally, the trio made their way to the back.

"Ruth has reached celebrity status," Gloria teased.

"Nah. Most of 'em are just being nosy. Sally Keane said she heard I overdosed," Ruth huffed. "Can you imagine that? Overdose on what?"

"Rose's potion," Margaret joked.

Ruth gave her a dark look and sank into an empty chair. "It had nothing to do with Rose's potion and everything to do with me trying to act like I'm eighteen again."

Dot stood. "I better get back to work. Do you all know what you want to eat?"

"I'm going to wait for Paul," Gloria said.

Ruth patted her stomach. "Chicken 'n dumplings."

"Make it two," Margaret said.

"I'll make it easy on you. Make it three," Lucy chimed in.

"Three chicken 'n dumplings coming up." Dot squeezed Ruth's shoulder. "We're glad you're all right."

After Dot left, Ruth cleared her throat. "While I was in the hospital bed twiddling my thumbs, I was thinking about Amy Mahoney and where her body was found."

"Did you remember something?" Gloria asked.

"No, but we need to get back inside the convention center," Ruth said. "I'm beginning to suspect it wasn't an inside job after all."

Chapter 12

"What do you mean - it might not have been an inside job?" Margaret shook her head.

"As in – inside the maze. I'm beginning to wonder if it might have been someone other than a contestant." Ruth leaned forward. "Think about it. Always suspect the least suspect. Of course, the most obvious suspects would be the other contestants."

"Motive and opportunity," Lucy said.

"Couple that with the online snipes Ruth and Amy Mahoney took at each other, not to mention the woman knocking Ruth down in front of everyone at the end of the first round of competition, Ruth is the most logical suspect," Gloria said.

"Well, we know Mahoney's uncle is the show's production manager, which in my opinion should be against the rules and something I plan to research."

"I did a little digging around when I got home," Gloria said. "After you told me about the link between Mahoney and the show's production manager, I tracked down the Dash for Cash show staff and found out something very interesting."

"There's another link," Ruth guessed.

"I believe so. There's another contestant. Baexter is his last name. I can't remember his first name."

"Travis?" Ruth asked.

"Yes, I think his name was Travis Baexter. I compared the list of contestants you gave me, with the show's staff. There's a Michael Baexter. He's the assistant producer's son. The spelling of the last name is uncommon. I'm wondering if they are somehow related."

"Maybe you should weasel your way into the Dash for Cash's studio instead of the convention center," Margaret said.

"The only problem with that is Travis Baexter was eliminated during the first round of competition," Ruth said.

"True. I guess we can scratch him." Gloria remembered something that hit her radar during her preliminary research. "Ruth, while I was snooping around the online chat board, I noted someone by the user name *dashboard* kept popping up. You mentioned you thought it might be one of the other contestants."

"Yes. I thought it might be Ivy Barnett."

"That username is stuck in my head. It's clever – Dash for Cash is the name of the show and board, as in online chat board. They took dash from the game show name and board from the board," Gloria said. "*Dashboard* posted yesterday, while the group was discussing Amy Mahoney's death. The person made several comments, mostly that the show was rigged to favor certain contestants."

"I'll have to check it out later to see if I can confirm the link between the two," Ruth said. "Still, I wouldn't mind taking another look around the convention center, scope out the layout of the place."

Rose arrived with bowls of food and set them in front of Lucy, Margaret and Ruth. "Now be careful. The chicken 'n dumplings are piping hot."

"Thanks for the warning, Rose," Margaret said. "Are you and Dot going to be able to join us?"

"Yeah, in a minute. Dot's gotta finish up a few orders, and then we'll have time to chit chat."

The women waited for Rose to make her way to another table and then bowed their heads to pray, thanking God that Ruth was all right. As they said amen, Gloria added a silent prayer of thanks for Dot's negative biopsy results.

Lucy reached for a roll. "I feel bad, eating in front of you." She handed the basket of bread to Gloria. "At least eat a roll while you wait for Paul."

"Okay." Gloria reached for a warm roll and tore off a chunk. "If you want to check out the convention center, we're going to have to figure out a way to get inside."

Ruth ladled a large spoonful of chicken 'n dumplings from the bowl and blew on the food to cool it before easing the spoon into her mouth. "I know. We can't just barge in there, tell them I'm a suspect in Mahoney's murder and demand that they let us look around."

She dipped her spoon in the bowl again. "I...almost have an idea. Give me a minute." She continued eating her food, half listening as the others continued discussing the case.

"I think I have it." Ruth grabbed her napkin and dabbed at the corners of her mouth before tossing it next to her bowl. "I've got to make a quick phone call."

She wiggled out of her chair and hurried out of the restaurant, to the front sidewalk where Gloria watched as she pulled her cell phone from her jacket pocket. "I wonder who she's calling."

"Could be anyone," Margaret remarked. "That woman has more connections than AT&T."

Ruth returned moments later, beaming from ear to ear. "It's all set. I'm going to run the downtown Grand Rapids delivery route Saturday morning, the one that includes deliveries to the convention center. "I need a volunteer to go with me."

Although Ruth asked for volunteers, she locked eyes with Gloria. "Me?" Gloria squeaked. "Well, at least it doesn't involve breaking and entering."

"There will be a teensy smidgen of deception." Ruth resumed her spot at the table and picked up her napkin.

"What kind of deception?" Gloria asked suspiciously.

Ruth lowered her head and mumbled.

"I didn't catch that," Gloria said.

"You'll need to wear a uniform and pretend you're working with me."

"Isn't it illegal, posing as a federal employee?" Margaret asked.

"Well." Ruth rubbed her chin. "It's kind of a gray area since I plan to remove the official USPS emblem from the outfit, and I won't specifically state that you're a United States Postal worker."

Lucy snorted. "You're going to remove the patches on one of your work uniforms so Gloria can accompany you to the convention center and help you snoop?"

"In a nutshell. It will look suspicious if someone wearing street clothes comes with me. All I'm going to say is that Gloria is helping me for the day."

"Oh boy." Gloria rolled her eyes.

"It'll be a piece of cake. I'll make small talk with whoever takes the delivery while Gloria excuses herself for a trip to the restroom. Instead of heading to the restroom, she'll sneak into the convention hall to have a look around."

"It will take time," Gloria objected. "Why don't you do the scoping out and I'll do the distracting?"

"It's a thought," Ruth said. "I just need to make sure we don't in any way, explicitly state you're a federal employee."

"I see more holes in this plot than Swiss cheese," Margaret grunted.

"Me too," Gloria said.

"I need to get back in there. Ruben agreed to let me run the route, and that's the only way we're gonna get in there without it looking suspicious."

"Have you checked out the convention center's calendar of events? Maybe there's a quilting show or home and garden expo going on. We can attend the show and check it out without ever raising an ounce of suspicion," Gloria said.

"Great idea. I'll see what I can find." Lucy whipped her cell phone out of her pocket and tapped the screen. "There's an Empowered Communities Conference starting tomorrow."

"Sounds political," Margaret said.

"I think you're right," Lucy said. "There will be a social justice speaker as well as representatives from the ACLU."

"I rest my case."

"That's out," Gloria said. "I don't want to become involved in politics. Anything else, Lucy?"

"Yeah. There's an Amway Platinum Members Conference starting Monday, but nothing else until after Thanksgiving."

"I guess it means I'm on the hook," Gloria said. "When are we going?"

"Saturday morning."

"My only day to sleep in now that Paul is working full-time," Gloria grumbled, before noting the pleading look on Ruth's face. "All right. I'll go with you. If I end up in jail, you have to promise to post my bail."

"Agreed." Ruth set her spoon on the bowl, looking a little pale.

Margaret must've noticed because she abruptly stood. "We need to get Ruth home."

"I am a little tired." Ruth pushed her bowl back. "Thank you all for hunting me down, for breaking into my house...Lucy...for calling an ambulance."

"We love you Ruth." Gloria sprang from her chair, ran around the table and gave Ruth a quick hug. "You would do the same for us."

"Without a doubt."

Lucy, Margaret and Ruth passed Paul on the way out, and he briefly chatted with them before catching his wife's eye and making his way across the restaurant. "Did you eat already?"

"Nope. I was waiting for you."

Paul gave his wife a quick kiss and then slid into the chair Margaret had vacated. "Whew. What a long day. I don't know if I'm feeling my age or I'm not used to working full shifts anymore."

"Maybe it's a little of both," Gloria said.

Dot made her way over. "Rats, I missed the girls. I wanted to tell them good-bye and also tell Ruth how happy I was that she's okay."

"Is something wrong with Ruth?" Paul asked.

Gloria sucked in a breath. "I think my day may have been just as long as yours. Ruth took a ride to the hospital earlier today. She left the post office during her break this morning to run home and grab something to eat. When she got there, she passed out."

Dot shoved a fist on her hip. "Lucy picked the lock on Ruth's back door, and when she and Gloria got inside and found Ruth unconscious, they called an ambulance."

"And they let her out of the hospital already?"

"They ran a bunch of tests. The doctors couldn't pinpoint a reason for her collapse, other than she hadn't eaten anything."

"Hypoglycemia," Paul guessed.

"Maybe," Gloria said.

Dot pulled her order pad from her pocket. "What can I get for you, Paul?"

"I'll have a Coke." He eyed a tray full of food that passed by. "Did I just see your chicken 'n dumplings?"

"Yep."

"I'll have the chicken 'n dumplings," Paul said.

"Make it two," Gloria said.

Dot gave them a thumbs up. "Got it. I'll bring you a basket of bread, too."

Paul waited until Dot stopped to chat with diners at another table. "You probably didn't have time to work on Ruth's investigation with all of that going on."

"I did, for a little while. Eleanor, Andrea and I also stopped by Lucy's place to do a little target practice. It's been quite the day. You said you were tired. Are you going to give it a couple more days before deciding to continue working through the holiday season?"

"Yeah."

Ray returned with Paul's glass of Coke, and they chatted briefly before Ray left. "I know the agreement was I wouldn't work weekends, but one of the other security guard's wives is going in for a C-section to deliver their baby, and he needs someone to cover for the weekend."

"What day?"

"Days. Both Saturday and Sunday. In exchange, I'll have tomorrow off plus another day sometime later in the week."

"Sure," Gloria nodded. "That will be all right. I mean, what could you say? Sorry I can't help you out."

"My sentiments exactly. Maybe you can go hang out with one of the girls or spend some time with Tyler and Ryan this weekend."

Gloria sucked in a breath. "I'll have to wait and see. I think I may already have plans for Saturday."

Chapter 13

"Just tuck it in. No one is going to notice if it's a little too big," Ruth said.

Gloria shoved the shirttails in the front of the pants, all the while scowling at her friend. "I'm still on the fence about this whole plan."

"It's not like you're breaking the law. All you have to do is tag along with me. We head to the convention center office. While I'm delivering the mail, you ask if you can use the restroom. I'll distract the convention center employee or employees while you scope out the auditorium. It's an airtight plan. There's no way you'll get caught."

"Famous last words," Gloria muttered.

Ruth exited the delivery truck and made her way to the back where she stacked several boxes on top of the handcart and wheeled it toward the curb.

Gloria fell into step. "Why not research the layout of the convention center online?"

"I already tried. All it shows is a single photo of the hall. You can't see anything."

"This is going to be a one-time deal," Gloria said. "Refresh my memory. Remind me what I'm looking for."

They reached the entrance to the convention center and Ruth stopped abruptly. "Do you remember the exact location of where the maze was set up?"

Gloria briefly closed her eyes and nodded. "Yes. It was to the right of the entrance doors and if I recall correctly, it took up almost half of the hall."

"Right. Amy Mahoney's body was found in the back, the farthest away from the spectators. My theory is someone may have gained access to the maze via a connecting portable panel. Those things snap together like Legos. If my theory holds water, the area has a blind spot, perfect for sneaking in and out undetected. After the killer slipped into the maze, they waited for Mahoney to come their way. Remember, all of the final contestants were blindfolded. We wouldn't have seen anyone. She was injected with a lethal dose of morphine and then the killer snuck back out the way they came in."

Ruth shifted the handcart to the side while Gloria held the door open.

"I see lights on over there." Ruth tipped the cart and headed toward the door, her rubber-soled shoes squeaking on the polished tile floors.

Gloria's heart began to race when they reached a door marked "Convention Center Office." Ruth rapped lightly and pushed the door open before the women stepped inside.

A young man, seated at a desk not far from the entrance, made his way to the counter. "Is Ruben off today?"

"Yes," Ruth nodded. "I'm filling in for him. I have several boxes I need you to sign for."

"Great." The man reached for the box on top while Ruth consulted her mobile delivery device. "There's one package in here that needs a signature." She gave Gloria a quick glance.

"I...uh." Gloria cleared her throat. "Do you have a nearby restroom I might use?"

"Sure." The man walked to the office door and pointed down the hall. "It's down the hall on the right. If you reach the Grand River Hall, you've gone too far."

"Isn't that the one where the Dash for Cash contest was held the other day? Heard some woman died," Ruth said.

"Yeah. It was in the Grand River Hall, one of our larger halls. From what I was told, the authorities are still investigating."

Gloria thanked the man and slipped out of the office. She walked as fast as she dared, passing by the restrooms and making a beeline for the doors marked, 'Grand River Hall.' When she reached the double doors, she pulled on both handles, but the doors were locked.

With a furtive glance behind her, she quickly stepped into a smaller, side corridor, which ran alongside the hall.

Several sets of doors lined the corridor and she jogged to the first set she found. The door was locked, so she ran to the next one, pulled it open and peered into the pitch-black darkness.

"Great." Gloria ran both hands along the wall, fumbling for the light switch. She found the switch and flipped it on.

Her eyes scanned the hall as she attempted to gather her bearings and remember the exact location of the maze. As luck would have it, it had been on the other side of the room. She sprinted to the other side.

A row of doors lined the long wall, what Ruth had deemed the blind area, near the back of the maze. Gloria pushed the first door open and stuck her head in a small room filled with electrical panels. She opened the second door. It was a closet, filled with mop buckets and cleaning supplies.

There was one more door, in the far corner. Gloria eased the supply closet door closed and dashed to the door, pushing it open. It led to another corridor, identical to the one on the other side she'd just left.

Determined to find out where it led, she flipped the main hall lights off and crept into the corridor.

To the left and at the end of the corridor was a large, open area. Gloria shifted her gaze and studied the door on the right marked "Exit." Her armpits began to sweat as she made her way to the exit door and reached for the bar to push it open.

"Here goes nothing." Gloria squeezed her eyes shut and prayed it wasn't an emergency exit, and that it wouldn't trigger an alarm. She sucked in a breath and pushed the door open.

Thankfully, the only sound she heard was the *swoosh* of the door sweep brushing against the concrete pad.

Gloria stepped into a back alley. To the right and roughly ten feet from the door was a dumpster. To the left was a delivery bay and beyond that, a parking lot.

Gloria pressed her foot against the bottom of the door to hold it open. She plucked her cell phone from her back pocket, turned it on and took several pictures, including one of the delivery bay as well as the dumpster. She backed into the corridor and snapped a picture of the door before hurrying to the other end.

When she reached the end of the corridor, she veered to the left, once again passing by the main entrance to Grand River Hall as she retraced her steps, making her way back to the office.

She spotted Ruth through the window with her elbow propped on the counter. Gloria pushed the door open and stepped inside the office.

"I told Ruben, you better make sure you have your I's dotted and your t's crossed if you don't want to get called to the boss' office for not having your paperwork signed." She stopped talking and turned to Gloria. "What happened to you?"

Gloria said the first thing that popped into her head. "I think the spicy enchilada I ate for dinner last night came back to haunt me."

Ruth curled her lip. "A little too much TMI, if you know what I mean." She turned to the man. "It was nice chatting with you Dan."

Gloria smiled at the man and followed Ruth out of the office. "Did I take too long?"

"Nope. The timing was near perfect." Ruth rolled the handcart into the back of the delivery truck and then climbed into the driver's seat. "Well?"

"It took me a couple of tries to find an unlocked door leading into the convention center hall. Your theory was spot on. There were several doors on the far side of the room, blind spots if you will, where it would've been easy for someone to slip into the area unseen."

"Were you able to find out where they led?" Ruth asked.

"No. I was in a hurry to get back, so I didn't have time to check it out."

"You didn't?" Ruth gasped. "We just wasted our time."

"I'm kidding." Gloria waved a hand. "Of course I did."

"And?"

"It led to a small corridor, a few feet away from an exit door. On the other side of the exit door was a loading dock, a dumpster and beyond that, a parking lot."

"If I drove around the building, do you think you would be able to find it?" Ruth asked.

"I can do one better." Gloria pulled her cell phone from her pocket and waved it triumphantly in the air. "I took pictures."

Ruth beamed. "Good girl. I'd still like to get a visual on it myself."

"Of course you would." Gloria pointed to the right. "I think if we head this way, I should be able to locate the exit."

"I feel like we may be onto something." Ruth shifted the delivery truck into drive, and they crept through the parking lot as they searched for the exit.

The first delivery bay and dumpster she spotted matched what Gloria remembered seeing. The only thing missing was a parking lot. "Keep going. We're looking for a dumpster, a loading dock and a parking lot."

"I see one up ahead." Ruth pressed her foot on the gas pedal, and they sped toward the spot.

"This could be it. There's another one over there. It looks about the same."

"Great." Ruth slowed the delivery truck. "We're back to square one."

"Not necessarily." Gloria tapped her cell phone screen and scrolled through the pictures. "I should've brought my reading glasses."

Ruth held out her hand. "Here. Let me look."

Gloria handed her the phone and Ruth studied the screen. "There's some sort of signage on the side of the dumpster and a couple of empty pallets propped up against the side of the loading dock." Ruth studied the dock to her left. "This isn't it. See? No pallets."

"Good eye, Ruth."

Ruth set the phone in her lap, and they drove past the first loading dock, to the next one. "I see pallets."

"And I see another loading area."

Ruth drove on and they approached the third dock. Again, there were no pallets. "It has to be the one we just passed."

"Based on the layout of the convention center and the location of the Grand River Hall, the exit would be in this vicinity," Gloria said. "Let's go back and check it out."

Ruth spun the wheel and steered the delivery truck back to the second bay. She slowed to a stop and then picked up Gloria's phone, studying the screen. "I'm almost positive this is it." She shifted into park and reached for the door handle.

"You're going to get out?" Gloria asked.

"That's why we're here. We need to take a closer look. Maybe there's a clue."

"I suppose." Gloria reluctantly reached for the door handle.

"There's no one around. Dan told me they were light on staff today."

"What if he's wrong?" Gloria sucked in a breath. "Let's do this before I change my mind."

The women exited the vehicle and cautiously approached the loading area. The dock was empty, except for a few scraps of paper that had collected in the corner near the overhead door.

Ruth kicked one of the pallets with the tip of her shoe and then turned her attention to the dumpster. "I wonder if there's anything of interest in here." She didn't wait for Gloria to reply and grasped the edge of one of the openings, pushing herself up so that she was teetering on a small ledge.

"What are you doing?" Gloria hissed.

"Searching for clues," Ruth said. "It would go a lot faster if you headed to the other side to see if you can see anything."

"Why not? Dumpster diving has always been on my bucket list."

Ruth grinned. "I owe you one."

"Or two." Gloria made her way to the other side of the dumpster. Using both hands, she grabbed the bottom of the opening and pulled herself up, balancing her left foot on the ledge. The smell of rotting cabbage wafted up, and Gloria began to gag.

"Breathe through your mouth."

"With my luck, something will fly into it." Gloria opened her mouth and forced herself to focus on the task at hand. Her eyes narrowed as she studied the contents of the dumpster. There were empty food wrappers, some construction debris and several bags of trash.

Ruth adjusted her grip. "Do you still have your phone?"

"Yeah. It's in my jacket pocket."

"Can you turn it on? We can use the light to see."

"Sure, but if I lose my balance and fall in, you're going to pull me out."

"It's a deal," Ruth said.

Gloria tightened her grip and shifted her foot for better balance. She stuck her free hand in her jacket pocket and pulled out her cell phone. She tapped the flashlight icon and stuck it inside the dumpster.

"That's much better," Ruth said.

Gloria ran the light along the perimeter of the bin.

"Ah, I think I see something," Ruth said.

Whoop...whoop

"What was that?" Gloria jerked her head around. Jogging towards them was a uniformed man. "It's a cop."

Chapter 14

The man lifted a bullhorn. "Put down the trash and step away from the dumpster!"

"Oh brother," Ruth groaned. "It's worse than a cop...it's a cop wannabe, a security guard. No offense to Paul, of course."

"Of course," Gloria gingerly stepped onto the ground while Ruth released her grip and hopped off the dumpster. "What's the problem?"

The guard kept one hand on his stun gun and the other on the bullhorn. "You're trespassing."

"We're here for a legitimate reason. I'm a United States Postal worker." Ruth tapped her name tag. "I just finished delivering mail to the office, was driving by and thought I spotted a recycle bin."

"This dumpster is off limits," he retorted.

"By whose authority?" Ruth challenged.

Gloria's eyes widened. *What was Ruth doing?*

"My authority." The guard pointed at his badge. "I'm in charge of security."

"For real?" Ruth leaned forward. "Your badge looks like it came out of a bubble gum machine."

"Ruth..." Gloria said.

"I ought to call the cops," the guard said.

"And tell them what? Two little old ladies were looking inside a garbage dumpster? They would laugh you right out of your uniform."

"I could have you arrested under Penal Code 750.356." The security guard reached for his radio and visions of a concrete block cell filled Gloria's head. *Wait until the cops found out she was impersonating a government worker!*

Her eyes darted to the postal delivery truck as she tried to gauge her odds of outrunning the security guard. They weren't good.

Ruth cleared her throat. "Penal Code 750.356 pertains to larceny. So you're saying that we're stealing garbage?"

The guard stiffened his back. "How do I know you're not trying to steal the dumpster?"

"Oh please...now you sound ridiculous. How on earth are two women going to get an eight-foot dumpster on top of a postal delivery truck? Just listen to what you're saying."

"We'll just see about that." The guard plucked his radio from his belt as he glared at Ruth.

"Good. Call the cops. I'll tell them you're violating Penal Code Section 750.411h, stalking."

"I-I'm not stalking you," the guard stuttered.

"It's your word against ours." Ruth pointed at Gloria, and Gloria started to shake her head, wishing the ground would open up and swallow her.

She watched in disbelief as the guard slowly replaced the radio. "Maybe this was all just a misunderstanding. I'm going to give you the benefit of the doubt. Our recycle bin is around the next corner. I'll be keeping an eye on you, so don't try anything funny."

"Great." Ruth turned to go. "I thought you might see things my way." She motioned to Gloria, and the women sauntered to the delivery truck before climbing inside.

The guard watched them like a hawk as Ruth steered the vehicle along the back of the building, stopping next to a bin marked 'recycle.' "I guess I better find something to throw away since ole eagle eye is still watching us."

"I'll wait here," Gloria said.

Ruth rummaged around in the back and removed a couple of small boxes before walking over to the bin and tossing them inside. She gave the security guard a jaunty wave and then made her way back inside the vehicle. "That was a close one."

"A little too close," Gloria said. "If he had called the cops, we would've been arrested, or at least *I* would've been arrested."

"He was bluffing." Ruth waved her hand. "Did you see how he backed down when I told him I was going to claim stalking charges? The man has a rap sheet a mile long. Mark my words."

"Don't they run background checks on security guards?"

"One would think so, but maybe this clown slipped through the cracks."

Gloria changed the subject. "What did you find in the bin before the security guard scared us half to death?"

"I'm almost certain I spotted a blonde wig."

"Long hair? Short hair?"

"It was short hair and to be honest, it could've passed for a woman's blonde wig or possibly even a man's wig."

"There's no proof Amy Mahoney's killer tossed the wig in the dumpster. It could've been anyone...any employee. The contest was three days ago," Gloria pointed out. "What are the chances of the killer tossing the wig inside the dumpster three days ago and it's still sitting on top?"

"Judging by the smell inside the dumpster, the trash has been there for a while. It would depend on whether there were any other events at the convention center during the last couple of days. If the Grand River Hall sat vacant since the Dash for Cash eliminations, then I would say it's a pretty safe bet it was thrown in there the day of the contest."

"Point taken," Gloria said. "Let me see if I can take a look at this month's calendar of events again." She turned her cell phone on and logged onto the internet before typing in the Grand Rapids Convention Center. She clicked on the calendar of events.

"It appears there was a bridal show the other day, but nothing in between. Still, it doesn't mean the bridal show was inside the same hall. The convention center has several large halls."

Ruth made an unexpected sharp turn and Gloria's head bumped the passenger window. "What are you doing?"

"I'm going back for the wig. It's potential evidence," Ruth said. "Reach into my purse and grab a clean pair of rubber gloves out of the bag."

"You keep rubber gloves in your purse?" Gloria shook her head. "Never mind. Of course you do." She located the package of gloves and pulled two out.

"Can you take over for me for a minute? We need to do a drive by. If the security guard isn't around, I'll hop out and grab the wig."

"You must be itching to check out the inside of a jail cell," Gloria said.

"I'm not going to jail for taking something from a dumpster."

"Okay, you'll get fined, and *I'll* go to jail for stealing a government vehicle and impersonating a federal worker."

"You worry too much." Ruth shifted into park and hurried to the passenger side.

Gloria scrambled across her seat and slid behind the wheel. She glanced in the rearview mirror before steering the vehicle towards the dumpster area. "I have no idea how you talk me into some of this stuff."

"You only have yourself to blame. You taught me everything I know about covert operations...well, almost everything." Ruth kept one hand on the door handle and peered out the front windshield. "Slow down."

Gloria took her foot off the gas pedal and opened her mouth to ask Ruth to let her know where she wanted her to stop, but it was too late.

Ruth had already jumped out of the moving vehicle and began jogging toward the dumpster.

"I hope she knows what she's doing." Gloria glanced anxiously in the side mirror, certain the security guard would reappear at any moment, brandishing his Taser gun. She shifted her gaze and watched as Ruth leaped onto the ledge of the dumpster and dove through the opening. She didn't completely clear the opening and her feet dangled in the air.

"Uh-oh." Gloria reached for the handle, ready to rescue her friend, but Ruth quickly recovered.

She teetered in mid-air before swinging her feet back and forth, as she wiggled her way out. Ruth hopped off the ledge, triumphantly waving the wig in the air.

"I got it." Ruth crawled into the passenger seat. "Piece of cake." She reached behind her, grabbed a priority mail shipping envelope and shoved the wig inside. She peeled off the strip and sealed it shut before removing her gloves.

"It may have all been for nothing. Remember, we're still not sure it was someone on the outside. What if it was another of the final contestants?"

Gloria drove to the front of the parking lot and wiggled out of the driver's seat. "Don't forget to send me a copy of the video of the inside of the maze you took using your handy dandy recording watch."

"I've been meaning to. Now that we have more clues, including a possible path the killer or killers used to gain access to the maze area without being spotted, the video might be more useful."

Ruth made a quick detour, stopping at a gas station, not far from the post office where Gloria removed the post office uniform and slipped into her own clothes.

The downtown Grand Rapids post office was a sprawling structure, covering almost an entire city block. Ruth parked the delivery truck while Gloria waited in her friend's van for her to turn in her paperwork.

She returned and climbed into the driver's seat. "Thanks for going with me today, Gloria."

"You're welcome. Have you heard what you'll have to do during the Dash for Cash competition?" Gloria remembered from one of the few times she'd watched that one of the events involved balancing on an exercise ball while the contestant attempted to write their name on a pad of paper.

"Yeah, but only one of the events. I can't believe the winners chose the dreadmill competition."

"Dreadmill?"

"A modified version of walking on a treadmill," Ruth said. "Margaret is going to let me borrow her treadmill so I can practice."

"Walking on a treadmill sounds like a walk in the park."

"It's not a treadmill, it's a *dreadmill*," Ruth said. "You walk on the dreadmill while performing a task, yet to be revealed."

"Are you sure all of this is worth being on Dash for Cash?"

"If I make it to the final round with a chance to compete in the Dash for Cash, then the answer is yes. I mean, I don't need a trip to Vegas or a set of new living room furniture. I want to win the top prize."

"Which is? Maybe you told me, but I already forgot."

"It's a shot at the cash cube money machine." Ruth went on to explain it was a clear, Plexiglas booth. "I've done my research. They use a powerful 1 HP deluxe blower. It connects to the back of the booth and circulates the bills/money once the contestant is inside."

Ruth continued. "Participants are not allowed to trap the bills against the ceiling of the structure, the walls or even their own body. It's also a no-no to bend at the waist or knees to scoop the bills off the bottom."

"You're only able to keep what you grab while it's blowing in your face?" Gloria asked.

"That's a possible scenario. I'm hoping it's the one where they affix a small box to the front of the booth, and the goal is to shove as much cash as possible into the box before the buzzer sounds."

Ruth slowed at the yield sign, looking both ways before continuing. "I've been studying some YouTube videos and have lined up several strategies, depending on the type of cash booth they use."

"After all you've gone through, I hope you get a chance to try them out," Gloria said. She grew quiet as she stared out the passenger side window. The authorities had no proof Ruth was involved in Amy Mahoney's death. Sure, it didn't look good, but there was no way they could pin it on her friend.

She thought about the contestant who was related to one of the show's producers. Amy Mahoney also had connections to the television show's staff. What were the chances of two people in the same group being related? Surely, there must be some sort of rule against family members being allowed to compete. Gloria made a mental note to research it.

Then, there was *dashboard*, aka Ivy Barnett, the person who posted in the contestant forum. The poster obviously knew a lot about the show.

Perhaps Ruth's video recording would be able to shed some light on what exactly happened inside the maze and the moments leading up to Amy Mahoney's lethal injection.

"...and then I'm going to run by Rose's to pick up another dose of her special concoction."

"I'm sorry Ruth," Gloria said. "I was working on putting the puzzle pieces together."

"It's okay. I said I'll drop you off at home, and then I'm going to swing by Rose's place to pick up more of her energy mix."

Ruth pulled into Gloria's drive. "Mally is waiting for you."

"Yes, she is." Gloria could see Mally's snout pressed firmly against the door's glass pane. "As soon as I take Mally for a walk, I'm going to lay out all of the clues...the list of contestants, study your video as soon as you send it to me, and take another look at the online chat. I suspect there are clues hidden inside the chat group. I just have to figure out what they are."

"I plan to do the same," Ruth said. "Maybe after today's investigation, we'll be able to connect at least a few of the dots. See you at church in the morning?"

"I'll be there. Paul is working all day tomorrow," Gloria said. She started to close the door and then had a sudden thought. "I know it's short notice, but why don't I have a Sunday potluck here at my place after visiting the shut-ins?"

"I'm in," Ruth said. "I have this amazing recipe for creamy chicken and wild rice soup. It's delish."

"I've got a few roasting chickens I need to use up," Gloria said. "How does three o'clock sound?"

"Works for me," Ruth said. "Maybe the others will be able to join us; we can put our heads together and figure out who killed Mahoney."

"I was thinking the same thing. I'll start calling everyone when I get inside. You can check with Rose when you see her."

"Will do. Thanks again for tagging along." Ruth raised a hand and saluted Gloria before driving off.

Mally didn't give Gloria a chance to step inside before she ran past her and out into the yard.

Gloria trailed behind, her mind on the mystery. There were so many different directions it could go. The most obvious suspects were the contestants, but then, maybe it was too obvious. Then there was the Dash for Cash staff members.

She needed to concentrate on the online chat group. Perhaps the killer was even on the chat board, noticed how Ruth and Amy Mahoney were at odds, and used it to their advantage to cast suspicion on Ruth.

After Mally finished patrolling the perimeter of the property, she inspected what was left of the garden, and then disappeared behind the back of the house before circling around the front.

Gloria's first task was to call her friends to invite them to the potluck. She decided to include Eleanor, since she had been a part of the preliminary investigation. Eleanor didn't answer and Gloria left a message.

Her next call was to Lucy. "Hi Gloria. How did your undercover operation turn out?"

"It almost went off without a hitch."

"Almost," Lucy laughed. "At least you're not in jail."

"No, not jail, although it was touch and go at one point. I almost landed in the bottom of a dumpster."

"You went dumpster diving?"

"Sort of. It's a long story," Gloria sighed. "The reason I'm calling is to invite you to an impromptu potluck at my place at three o'clock tomorrow after the shut-in visits."

"It sounds like fun. I have a few errands to run, but I can do them after church," Lucy said. "What would you like me to bring?"

Gloria told her she was roasting chickens and Ruth was bringing homemade chicken and wild rice soup. "Bring whatever you want."

"I have a whole bag of red potatoes I need to use. I'll make a pan of rosemary and garlic roasted red potatoes."

"That sounds yummy," Gloria said. "I'll fill everyone in on what happened today and what Ruth and I found out tomorrow."

"Margaret is here with me at the property. Would you like me to invite her?"

"Of course. It will save me a phone call."

"Hang on." Lucy's voice grew muffled and she came back on the line. "Margaret's in. She said to tell you she'll bring a batch of baked beans."

"I love Margaret's baked beans," Gloria said. "Now all I have left is to call Andrea and Dot."

She told Lucy good-bye and dialed Andrea's cell phone. Andrea said she'd love to come. Brian planned to work on a project at his lakefront home and then she asked if she could invite Alice.

"Of course. The more the merrier." Gloria rattled off what everyone else was bringing.

"I don't know what to bring," Andrea said.

"How about a dessert?"

"Good idea. I'll bring a dessert. I'm not sure yet what it will be. I'll come up with something." Gloria told Andrea good-bye and smiled as she hung up the phone.

The only person left was Dot, and when Gloria called the restaurant, Dot answered, but seemed distracted, so Gloria quickly extended the invitation and told her to think about it, that she didn't have to bring anything.

She promised to call Gloria back. After hanging up the phone, she fixed a sandwich, grabbed a bag of chips and carried them to the dining room.

Puddles waited until Gloria had settled onto the chair and then jumped onto her lap, sniffing the edge of the plate. "Ah. Is this what it takes to wake you up?" Gloria tore a small sliver of meat off and fed it to her cat.

Mally pawed the edge of the chair. "Of course, you get a bite too." Gloria tore off a bigger piece of meat and fed it to her pooch. "That's it. You both have food in your dishes."

Gloria took a big bite of her sandwich and turned the computer on, waiting for it to warm up. She slipped her reading glasses on and studied the printed list of contestants before logging onto her email account.

Ruth had remembered to send her a copy of the audio/video from her spy watch, and Gloria double clicked on the icon to open it. She enlarged the screen and turned up the volume as she focused her attention on the video.

The video bounced around, and it started to make Gloria dizzy again, so she closed her eyes and focused her attention on the audio. There were long stretches of heavy breathing, along with several grunting noises and a couple of loud thuds. Gloria guessed a blindfolded Ruth crashed into the wall as she attempted to navigate her way through the maze.

When she heard a small yelp, Gloria's eyes flew open. The yelp had not come from Ruth, Gloria would almost bet money on it.

Certain something had occurred that the audio caught, Gloria listened to it again, closing her eyes and straining an ear to make sure she'd heard correctly. It was there...the same yelp.

Gloria grabbed a chip and rewound the tape a third time, back to the three-minute mark. Her heart began to race as a shadowy figure flitted past Ruth.

Thirty seconds later, Gloria heard the yelp again.

Chapter 15

Gloria replayed the audio and video clip again to make sure she wasn't hearing things. She reached for her cell phone and sent Ruth a text to fill her in on what she'd heard.

What if there was a connection between whoever flitted past Ruth and the yelp? What if the yelp had come from Amy Mahoney?

She clicked out of the video and opened the Dash for Cash chat site. There was a lengthy discussion about Amy Mahoney's death and several of the users chimed in with their theory on what had happened inside the maze.

Ruth's name was mentioned a couple of times and how Mahoney had attacked Ruth, knocking her down during the first round of eliminations. No one outright accused Ruth of taking Mahoney out, but then they didn't defend her, either.

One poster mentioned Mahoney was rude and obnoxious, and while they didn't wish anyone dead, they could see how she might have made herself the target of an attack.

Another poster Gloria remembered from a previous conversation posed an interesting theory...what if the killer hadn't meant to inject a lethal dose of morphine, but meant to knock her out instead?

She had almost finished reading the entire thread when one post in particular caught her eye. It was a post by *play2win*...a single sentence stating perhaps there was more to Amy Mahoney's death than met the eye.

Gloria studied the list, the name *dashboard* with Ivy Barnett's name and a question mark next to it.

She still couldn't rule out Travis Baexter and decided to see if she could dig up a little more information on both Baexter and Mahoney. First, she needed to start with Amy Mahoney's uncle, Gerald Marsh.

There were several news stories about the man, his rise through the ranks until he reached the pinnacle of his career...production manager of the Multi-Media Entertainment Group. Gloria had to admit his lengthy list of credentials was impressive.

Below one of the articles was a brief Q&A. She skimmed through the list of questions until one in particular popped out:

Q. *If you could give one piece of advice to someone looking to break into the entertainment business, what would it be?*

A. *Work your connections. Connections will get you everywhere in life.*

Gloria leaned back and drummed her fingers on the desk. Connections. Of course, that's how Amy Mahoney was able to land a spot as a contestant...her connection to her uncle.

Michael Baexter was the next person Gloria began to research. He began his illustrious career in the entertainment field after a stint in the army, before leaving the army and taking a position as a stagehand, working behind the scenes, and then working his way up the ladder.

"An interesting work history," Gloria muttered under her breath. Nothing else caught her eye, so she clicked out of the screen and began researching Travis Baexter. She searched for several minutes without getting a single hit and then decided to find out if he had a social profile page.

She easily found Travis, noting he listed New York as his home state, but pointing out he'd been staying with family in Michigan for several months. He was an attractive young man, mid-20s if Gloria had to guess, with dark hair and eyes, and an engaging smile.

Gloria scrolled the screen to read some of his posts and his initial charm quickly vanished. The man boasted of his bevy of girlfriends, he complained he was having difficulty finding a job that suited him, insisting that people didn't take him seriously because he was good-looking.

"Oh brother." Gloria rolled her eyes. "He sounds like he's a little too full of himself."

The older posts were along the same lines, and Gloria grew weary of his whiny rants. Her father would have words of advice for Travis Baexter if he were still alive...to pull himself up by his bootstraps.

She moved on to researching the other remaining contestants' profiles, starting with the ones who had been eliminated during the first round. Deciding it was a waste of time until she was able to link the contestants' names to the chat board names and she needed Ruth's assistance, Gloria clicked out of the profiles.

Right now, the best bet for possible suspects was Ivy Barnett, Desiree Warner and Lane Jorgensen, the finalists, along with the chat board participants *dashboard* and *play2win*, who made the mysterious statement perhaps there was more to Mahoney's death than met the eye. If the poster meant it in the literal sense, perhaps Gloria needed to take a closer look at the poster.

She scooched her chair back and began to stroke Puddles' back. Her beloved cat was spending more time sleeping than he was awake. Gloria pushed aside the thought that Puddles was almost fourteen in human years and she knew from talking to the vet he'd reached his life expectancy.

At least down the road, when Puddles crossed the rainbow bridge, she'd know that she had loved him with all of her heart and he'd lived a good life. She wondered if pets went on to heaven, to wait for their beloved humans. It was something she'd pondered in the past and even researched, but never found a clear answer.

She had to believe a loving God, who wished to give us our hearts' desires, would have our most cherished companions waiting there for us.

Gloria set Puddles on the floor and then wandered into the kitchen. She began rummaging around in the freezer, searching for something to make for dinner and found a container of scalloped potatoes and ham she'd made a few weeks back.

"This'll do." She pulled the container from the freezer and set it on the counter before reaching back inside and grabbing a packet of freezer rolls.

She placed the rolls next to the scalloped potatoes and headed to the pantry to track down a side dish.

Mally, who had followed Gloria into the kitchen, began to whine at the door. "Are you ready to go out again already?" She grabbed a light jacket and followed Mally onto the porch.

Her pooch skittered down the steps and began sniffing around the lattice below the porch when a small movement near the barn caught Gloria's eye.

Mally must've noticed it, too, because she took off at a full gallop and raced to the side of the barn where she came to a screeching halt and began barking.

Concerned Mally had cornered a small bunny, or worse, a skunk, Gloria bolted down the steps and ran across the driveway. As she got close, she realized it wasn't a skunk or a bunny. It was a young cat with a smidge of white surrounding his nose and circling his small mouth.

"Mally, move back." Gloria nudged her dog away from the cat and gently picked it up. It let out the faintest meow Gloria had ever heard and she held him close, her fingers touching his small ribcage underneath. "You're starving, poor thing."

She carried the small animal inside. Thankfully, Puddles was nowhere in sight, so she set the cat on the floor and reached for Puddles' special dairy milk, something she'd picked up after the veterinarian suggested it.

Gloria poured a small amount in a saucer and then fresh water in another bowl. The cat lapped up all of the milk and then drank some of the water before sitting on his haunches and staring at Gloria, a look of hunger in his eyes.

"I can give you a little tuna." She opened a can of cat food and scooped a spoonful of tuna onto a small plate before setting it in front of him.

Mally, who sat watching the intruder carefully, let out a low whine. "You get a doggy treat for finding our new friend."

Gloria grabbed a handful of treats and fed them to Mally while the cat devoured the food and then licked the plate.

"I don't want to give you too much. I'm afraid your little tummy won't be able to handle it."

Gloria rinsed the dish in the sink and then placed it in the dishwasher. "Now what should I do with our unexpected visitor?"

It wasn't uncommon for strangers to drop strays at the farm. It had been several months since the last time, when she'd found a box, filled with a litter of kittens and had taken them to the *At Your Service* kennel and training center, where the kittens had been quickly adopted.

The cat Mally had found was still young, but beyond the kitten stage when most were adopted. His soulful eyes met Gloria's eyes, as if pleading with her.

With a quick inspection, she confirmed the visitor was a male and then cast a glance toward the dining room chair where Puddles was sound asleep and oblivious to the intruder who had invaded his territory.

Meow. The small cat let out a cry and Puddles lifted his head, blinking sleepily. When the newcomer did it a second time, Puddles sprang from the chair and paraded into the kitchen. He stopped in his tracks when he spotted the interloper.

Gloria almost scooped the cat up, but decided to wait for Puddles' reaction instead.

She remembered how Puddles took to Mally the moment they met. The two bonded and were forever best buds.

Puddles lowered onto his haunches and cautiously sniffed the air as he slowly approached the cat.

The cat took a tentative step forward and then stopped.

Puddles inched forward, creeping to within a foot of the cat and then stopped, never taking his eyes off the black ball of fur.

Gloria dropped to her knees and patted Puddles' head. "Look what I found out by the barn, Puddles. I don't think this kitty has a home. I gave him some of your food. I hope that's okay."

She continued petting her cat, talking to him in a soothing voice. "Is it okay if he stays with us until I can take him to *At Your Service*?"

The younger cat impatiently crept forward until the two were within striking distance. Puddles let out a throaty growl, causing the cat to retreat and he bumped into Gloria's leg.

Puddles stared at the small cat and then abruptly turned his head, as if completely disinterested in the intruder.

Meow. The cat let out a small whimper before flopping down on the floor and playfully swatting at Puddles.

Puddles yawned, as if bored, and stretched out on the floor.

"See? That wasn't so bad." Gloria crawled to the corner and scooped the kitty up, holding him close. "Puddles is pretty-laid back," she explained. "I wouldn't go overboard, trying to get him to play. Now, Mally on the other hand? She'll give you a run for your money.'

Mally, hearing her name tromped over and dropped down next to Gloria. The cat sniffed in Mally's direction and when Mally suddenly barked, the claws came out and the cat bolted out of Gloria's arm.

"Mally," Gloria scolded as she inspected the scratch on her arm. "You scared him half to death." She carried the cat to the spare bedroom, set him on the bed and then made her way out of the room, closing the door behind her.

Puddles and Mally promptly plopped down in front of the door to guard it.

Gloria returned to the kitchen and caught a glimpse of Paul, pulling into the drive. She stepped onto the porch. "You're home early."

"We were a little overstaffed, so they asked for volunteers to leave work early." Paul settled into the chair next to the door and began pulling off his work shoes.

"How was your day?"

"Not bad. I'm not nearly as tired as I was the first day." While Paul washed up, Gloria added some butter to the tops of the thawed rolls and then bumped up the oven temperature before gently sliding the pan of rolls into the oven.

With the rolls baking, she placed the dish of scalloped potatoes in the microwave and started the defrost cycle.

Paul snuck up behind his wife and kissed her neck as he slipped his arms around her waist. "I think it's time for another date night."

"I agree." Gloria turned to face her husband. "What do you have in mind?"

"I don't know. What I do know is it won't involve shopping," he joked. "How's the investigation into the contestant's death going?"

"I'm stuck. There are too many suspects and not enough clues." Gloria went on to explain she'd invited the girls over for a potluck lunch at three o'clock the following day and started to tell him about her online research when Mally barked, reminding Gloria they had a visitor. "I almost forgot."

She hurried to the spare bedroom door and shooed her pets away before opening it and sticking her head inside. The kitten was curled up on the bed, fast asleep. The sight of him tugged at Gloria's heartstrings. She gently picked him up and carried him into the kitchen.

"Mally found this little fella wandering around by the barn. He was starving."

Paul reached out to pat his head. "A stray. Are you going to take him to *At Your Service*?"

"That was my original plan, but just look at his adorable little face. I was thinking maybe we have room for one more."

As if on cue, the kitten began to purr, his whole body vibrating and he butted the top of his head on Gloria's chin. "See? He likes us."

"Well..." Paul sucked in a breath.

Chapter 16

Gloria tilted her head. "We get to keep the cat?"

"Of course." Paul grinned at his wife. "When was the last time I told you no?"

"Never." She bounced up on her tiptoes and kissed his lips. "That is one of the many reasons I love you. Now we must decide on a name."

"Samson," Gloria suggested. "Because he has a mighty purr."

"Or Houdini since he appeared out of nowhere."

Gloria studied the pixie face. He was cute as a button, and reminded her of Puddles when he was a kitten. She remembered Jake, a cat she'd had when she was young. The two were similar in color, except that Jake had been all black. This one had a touch of white. "He reminds me of a cat I once had. His name was Jake."

"Then Jake it is. If you like it, I like it."

"Jake?" Gloria scratched his ears to see what he thought. Jake tilted his head and nibbled on the side of her finger. "I think we've settled on a name."

The microwave beeped and Gloria set their new pet on the kitchen floor. Jake, secure in his new position, strolled to the other side of the room and stopped in front of Mally's doggie bed. He sniffed the edge and then crawled on top, circling it twice before settling in.

Mally scrambled onto all fours and promptly headed to her bed where she stared at Jake. She let out a low whine and pawed at the side.

Oblivious to Mally's disapproval, Jake opened one eye and then closed it again.

Paul set the table while Gloria stirred the scalloped potatoes and then opened the oven to check on the rolls. By the time Paul finished setting the table, the rolls were ready. Gloria eased the tray out of the oven and set them on top where she spread a generous pat of butter on each one.

The couple prayed over the food and began discussing the upcoming week and Paul's days off. They decided to take in a movie matinee, a new mystery Gloria had been patiently waiting to come to the local theaters.

The rest of the evening passed uneventfully and the couple turned in early. Before turning in for the night, Gloria managed to track down a makeshift litter box for Jake. She placed it, along with some food and water, in the bathroom and then shut him in.

Gloria awoke before the alarm clock sounded and crept out of the bedroom to start a pot of coffee. She made a quick detour to the bathroom and opened the door. Jake darted out of the room and began circling her ankles.

The litter box was intact and she was relieved that their new family member was already litter box trained, although his skills in covering his business left a little to be desired. She swept the spray of cat litter that dotted the floor and then slid the box next to the toilet.

She carried Jake's food and water dishes to the kitchen where she placed them next to Puddles and Mally's dishes, filling them all before turning her attention to breakfast. Fried bacon and scrambled eggs were in order, and she made a few extra eggs, scooping a spoonful onto each of her pets' dishes.

Paul stepped into the kitchen, his eyes falling to the three animals lined up side by side, eating from their food dishes. "I see everyone is getting along."

"For now," Gloria said. "Breakfast is ready." She refilled her coffee cup and filled one for Paul before reaching for her plate. "It will be strange being in church without you this morning."

Paul eased into an empty chair. "Working on Sundays is for the birds."

"It's for a good cause," Gloria reminded him. After Paul left, Gloria grabbed a skirt and long sleeve shirt and headed to the bathroom.

Jake followed her in. "I guess I'll have to leave the bathroom door ajar until we can figure out a permanent solution to the litter box situation."

She hung her clothes on the hook behind the door and a clean towel on the hook next to the shower before stripping off her pajamas and turning the shower on. Gloria had one foot in the tub, when the door flew open and Mally trotted in.

"Great. It's a party," she groaned as she climbed into the shower. "This is not going to work out." By the time she emerged from the shower, Puddles was perched on top of the toilet seat, Mally was sprawled out on the rug and Jake was roaming around the bathroom counter.

"Everyone out." She shooed her pets out of the bathroom and slipped into her skirt and shirt.

Gloria arrived at church right on time, and even managed to find an empty parking spot in the main parking lot. Most of the snowbirds had already headed south or west for the winter, and the weekly church attendance was starting to dwindle.

Lucy waved Gloria over and slid to the side to make room. "I wondered if you were going to make it."

"Paul left the house before daylight. I had plenty of time to make him breakfast and get ready."

Gloria felt a nudge on her shoulder. It was Margaret. Gloria and Lucy slid down and Margaret squeezed in next to them. "I talked to Ruth last night before I went to bed. She said she got a call from a Detective Pell. He's going to meet her at her place later this morning. He told her he had some new information in the Amy Mahoney case and wanted to discuss it with her."

"Maybe he has some good news." Gloria rubbed her chin. "If not, we have to figure out who is responsible for the woman's death. I poured over the clues yesterday. There are a few suspects, including a couple where I only know their online user names. I'm hoping Ruth can help me link them to the contestants."

"Maybe if we all work together, we can come up with some sort of plan," Lucy said. "I see Eleanor." She gave a small wave and a beaming Eleanor, who was seated at the piano, waved back.

"I agree." The choir assembled on the platform and the conversation ended as the congregation stood.

Pastor Nate's message focused on Christians shining their lights and being a beacon of light in the darkness of the world. He briefly mentioned the recent string of weather-related tragedies and asked the congregation to keep all of those affected in their prayers.

The pastor's key verse was Matthew 5:16:

"In the same way, let your light shine before others, that they may see your good deeds and glorify your Father in heaven."

It was a fitting verse and Gloria jotted it down, so that she could go back and read the accompanying verses later.

After the service ended, the women exited the building and gathered off to the side. It was Andrea's turn to deliver fruits and vegetables, along with baked goods to the shut-ins.

"Alice and I are bringing a taco salad and a pumpkin cream cheese roll to the potluck," Andrea said.

"Those both sound delicious," Dot said. "I'm bringing a roasted turkey and rolls."

"This get-together will be a good exercise in stretching our stomachs for the upcoming Thanksgiving feast," Gloria joked. She reminded them about the three o'clock lunch date and then headed to her car.

The early afternoon flew by as Gloria prepared for the potluck. Andrea and Alice were the first to arrive, and Gloria pointed to the section of her kitchen counter she'd cleared for the food.

Dot and Rose arrived moments later, setting their dishes next to Andrea and Alice's dishes. Lucy and Margaret were right behind them.

The last to arrive was Ruth. She breathlessly burst into the kitchen. "I'm sorry if I'm late. Detective Pell is hot to arrest someone for Amy Mahoney's murder, and I'm pretty sure he has his sights set on me."

"What did he say?"

"That he intercepted a message from someone on Amy Mahoney's cell phone. It was a threat and it appears to have been sent by one of the other contestants."

"That doesn't mean it was you," Margaret pointed out.

Ruth handed her dish to Gloria. "I'm the only one who got into it with Mahoney during the elimination round."

"Remember," Gloria said. "Mahoney mentioned something about 'you're both going down.' I still think if we can figure out who she meant by 'both' we'll be onto something."

She continued. "I spent some time poring over the list of contestants and trying to match them to the users in the chat group. Do you have any idea who *play2win* might be? I know you mentioned *dashboard* might be Ivy Barnett, at least that's what I wrote down."

"I'll have to take a look at it again," Ruth said.

"Let's eat first. We'll have plenty of time to sort it out later," Gloria said.

The women assembled in a circle and prayed over the food. They prayed for Andrea's baby, for all of their health and last, but not least, prayed they would be able to figure out who murdered Amy Mahoney.

Gloria waited for her friends to load their plates with roasted chicken and turkey, roasted red potatoes, baked beans, taco salad, and bowls of Ruth's creamy chicken and wild rice soup.

While they ate, the women discussed Dot's busy restaurant, the new shed Johnnie had installed in the backyard and Lucy and Margaret's rehab project.

"Where's Eleanor?" Ruth glanced around the table.

"She called me before church this morning and said she was having lunch with Pastor Nate and Sue to discuss this morning's music portion of the service and how it went," Gloria said.

After the women cleared the dishes, Gloria cut the pumpkin roll and set a stack of dessert plates next to the dish. A freshly brewed pot of coffee was in order, and after grabbing a slice of dessert, the women chatted about the weather, the upcoming holidays and the Sunday service.

"I'm stuffed," Gloria said. "We can clear the table and go over everything we have so far in the murder investigation."

The women made quick work of cleaning up while Ruth went over all that had happened from the moment she made it to the elimination rounds and joined the Dash for Cash chat group. She told them how Amy Mahoney joined the group and began mouthing off, telling everyone they didn't stand a chance against her and she was a shoe-in to win.

"Little did you know Mahoney was related to Gerald Marsh, the show's assistant producer," Margaret said.

"She was competing against Travis Baexter, whether she knew it or not," Gloria said. "I did a little research on Baexter. Not only is he Michael Baexter's son, he's a little too full of himself. Still, he's low on the totem pole of suspects. He didn't make it to the final round."

*

"Then there's Desiree Warner. She was bragging she was going to win," Ruth said.

Gloria snapped her fingers. "Desiree Warner. She's the fitness trainer and former corrections officer."

"Don't forget the wig we pulled from the dumpster outside the convention center," Ruth said.

"True." Gloria's eyes widened. "Ruth, remember when I told you I studied the video you recorded during the maze competition? I heard a noise. It was a yelp or a small scream. A woman's voice if I had to guess. It was right around the same time I spotted someone running by you in the maze. Think about it. How could someone run past you if they were wearing a blindfold?"

"Because they weren't wearing a blindfold?" Andrea asked.

"Or it was an evil spirit." Alice made a cross sign on her chest.

"The only evil spirit in the maze was the killer," Margaret said.

"I'm sure Rose has a potion for that," Dot joked.

"Darn tootin'," Rose said.

"Back to the matter at hand," Gloria said. "We need to figure out who murdered Amy Mahoney and who is letting Ruth take the rap for her death, but first I think we should all watch and listen to the recording to see if we all agree we hear the same thing."

The women followed Gloria into the dining room. They waited while she turned the computer on and clicked on the video Ruth had emailed her. The group grew quiet as Gloria played the portion of the audio where a figure darted past and then heard the yelp.

"I heard it," Lucy said.

"I saw someone plain as day," Margaret said.

"Clear as a bell and I saw it too," Dot said.

"We're all in agreement someone ran past Ruth, and it was followed by a woman's stifled yelp," Gloria said. "Now, we need to work on matching user names to contestants to try to narrow the list of suspects."

Ruth swiveled in her seat. "The only part you guys didn't hear...and I didn't hear it either, was in the very beginning when Mahoney told me we were both going down. For some reason, it didn't record."

"You're right," Lucy said. "I never heard it. Maybe she whispered it in your ear and it was so low, the recorder couldn't pick it up."

"That's the only thing I can think of." Ruth cleared her throat. "Before we get started, I have something else to tell you."

Chapter 17

"Well, actually two things. I received this email yesterday from the Dash for Cash production management team." Ruth reached into her purse, pulled out a single sheet of paper and handed it to Gloria. "I'll let you read it out loud so the others can hear."

Gloria took the sheet of paper and slipped her reading glasses on:

"Dear Ms. Carpenter,

The Multi-Media Entertainment Group takes the safety and welfare of our employees and contestants very seriously. In light of the recent unfortunate accident during the maze elimination phase, we have decided to postpone the taping of the upcoming show, of which you are a contestant.

Rest assured that as soon as the investigation into the unfortunate demise of one of the finalists has been completed, we will schedule Dash for Cash for the next available slot.

Thank you for your interest in the Multi-Media Entertainment Group and Dash for Cash.

Sincerely,

Victor Zagorski, Esq.

Manager, Business and Legal Affairs

Multi-Media Entertainment Group"

Gloria folded the sheet of paper and handed it back to Ruth. "It makes sense if you think about it. If they don't postpone the taping of the show, they're setting themselves up for some serious backlash from the public."

"A PR nightmare," Dot said.

"I guess you're right." Ruth's shoulders slumped. "Kenny said a bunch of suits were snooping around the post office yesterday, asking a lot of questions."

"Detectives?" Margaret asked.

"That would be my guess," Ruth said. "And, if all of that wasn't enough, Kenny said yesterday, while Gloria and I were doing a little intel at the convention center, he got an odd phone call. The caller was looking for me, and when Kenny told them I wasn't there, they asked if they could leave a message."

"What sort of message?"

"To watch my back because someone was trying to frame me for Mahoney's death," Ruth said.

"Was it a man or woman who called?" Andrea asked.

"Kenny said the caller was trying to disguise their voice. If he had to guess, it was a woman."

"Great." Lucy shook her head. "Not only are the police after you, but someone's trying to frame you for the murder."

"That is why we need to figure out who killed Mahoney," Gloria said. "We can scratch Ruth off the list. I'm guessing you already tried to track down the caller's number."

"I would if I could. There's no way to track the call. Modern technology hasn't reached the Belhaven post office yet."

"Before we get started, I need to let Mally out."

"I've got to use the restroom." Margaret headed to the bathroom.

"Wait! We have a new family member." It was too late. Margaret had opened the bathroom door and Jake hopped out. She bent down to pick him up. "Who's this?"

"His name is Jake."

"What an adorable kitten," Rose said. "I didn't know you were getting a new pet."

"Jake adopted us," Gloria said. "Mally found him out near the barn yesterday. My plan was to take him to *At Your Service*, but once I brought him inside and he started to warm up to us, we decided we couldn't part with him."

Gloria patted Jake's head. "He's wiggled his way into my heart already. So far, Puddles seems to tolerate him. I think Mally is having a harder time since Jake has staked claim to part of her doggy bed."

Alice rubbed Jake's paw. "He appears to be in good health. Perhaps a little on the skinny side. I'm sure you'll fatten him up."

"We're already working on it." Gloria made her way into the dining room and assembled all of the information she'd pulled together on Amy Mahoney's murder investigation. She logged onto the computer and pulled up the Dash for Cash chat group.

Ruth's eyes squinted as she stared at the screen. "It looks like there are a few new posts."

She reached for the list of contestants. "I'll get to work matching up the names." She shifted in her chair. "You said you were specifically trying to match the username *play2win*. I'm confident the user *play2win* is Desiree Warner."

"Maybe we should consider setting up a sting," Lucy said. "You know. Some way to try to trap the killer."

"I'll get started on trying to match the rest of the names." Ruth turned her attention to the computer, and the others congregated in the kitchen while Gloria brewed another pot of coffee. Motive and opportunity. The two words played over and over in her head.

Amy Mahoney seemed certain she was a shoe-in as a finalist and even bragged she would win a spot on the game show. The only way to be certain of that was if the show was rigged.

It was possible someone else...perhaps another contestant...knew the show was rigged and planned to take Mahoney out, leveling the playing

248

field. Still, to kill someone over a silly game show? Maybe the game show death was a cover for something else.

That was it. It had to be. The game show was a cover. Someone knew Ruth and Mahoney didn't care for each other, saw the show as an opportunity to take her out, all the while making it look as if the competition was the reason for her demise.

Gloria drifted into the dining room. "What if the game show was a cover? What if someone had it in for Mahoney and used the contest as an opportunity to take her out?" She slid into the chair next to Ruth. "Tell me everything you know about Amy Mahoney."

"She was rude, obnoxious, overbearing. From what you said, she had connections to the show, indicating it was rigged," Ruth added. "And she did not like me."

Gloria popped out of the chair. "There's something else that has been hovering in the back of my head and it's driving me crazy. Do you think you can find a previous episode of Dash for Cash on the internet?"

"Of course." Ruth beamed brightly. "I've studied every single episode." She turned her attention to the computer screen and after a few quick clicks, opened a new screen and hit the play button.

Gloria leaned over Ruth's shoulder, her eyes squinting as she studied the start of the show as the show's host, Bob Larker, called the contestants down to the stage. "That's it. You can stop the video. Ruth, who was the last contestant to become disqualified in the tag elimination?"

Ruth tapped the tip of her finger on the keyboard. "Let's see. I...don't remember. It was so crazy, and it didn't help that Mahoney knocked me flat on my back. Maybe we can tell from my video. I'll pull it up." She switched screens and opened a new window. "I was going to erase it since it was a cruddy recording and was pretty much useless."

"I'm glad that you didn't." Gloria's heart pounded as she began watching the tag elimination video. Whole sections of it were blurry.

"Stupid raincoat. I had no idea we were going to have to wear raincoats," Ruth said.

"Forward all of the way to the last couple of minutes," Gloria said.

Ruth dragged the bar to the right until there were only a couple of minutes left and then tapped the arrow. The tape began to play.

"There!" Gloria jabbed the screen. "Bingo!"

The women watched as Travis Baexter yanked the raincoat off and stomped out of the ring.

"Just as I suspected. I think Travis Baexter is the killer."

"How so?" Dot asked.

"I can't believe I didn't think of this before, although I'm sure the investigators are already on it. Think of it. There are five contestants on the show." Gloria lifted a finger and began ticking off the list. "Ruth, Ivy Barnett, Lane Jorgensen, Desiree Warner and Amy Mahoney, but Mahoney is out."

"Right," Ruth said. "That means one of the other contestants from the first round replaces Mahoney."

"Travis Baexter," Ruth and Gloria said in unison.

"But Baexter didn't have access to Amy," Gloria said.

"Unless he snuck in through a loose side panel and escaped out the back door," Ruth reminded Gloria.

"The first on the list is Desiree Warner aka *play2win*. Desiree is a straight shooter. Tall, athletic and a former corrections officer. Next is Lane Jorgensen. I don't know much about him.

He was a lurker on the boards, never commenting. I do know that he's young and from the Detroit area. The third person who made it to the finalists was Ivy Barnett. She's a professional game show player, bragging to anyone who would listen that she's been on several game shows."

"And you think her chat group username is *dashboard*?" Gloria asked.

"Yep," Ruth said. "I'm almost 100% certain Ivy Barnett's username is *dashboard*, the one who seems to have a lot of knowledge about the inner workings of game shows."

"It makes sense if what you say is true and Ivy is a professional game show contestant," Gloria said. "I'm not convinced that Travis acted alone. I think he had an accomplice, based on Mahoney's comment that you were both going down."

"Perhaps it was Desiree Warner, the former corrections officer, a good cop gone bad," Lucy said.

"No." Gloria shook her head. "*Play2win*, aka Desiree Warner, commented that there might be more to Mahoney's death than met the eye. If she was the killer, she wouldn't have made that comment."

"It could be the mystery man, Lane Jorgensen," Andrea pointed out. "He's flying under the radar."

"There is one more thing that might move Ivy Barnett to the top of the list as a potential accomplice," Ruth said. "She's been bragging if she made it onto the Dash for Cash show, she would be in the running to make it into the Guinness Book of World Records for the number of game shows participated in."

"I'll add my two cents. I think Ivy was the one who called the post office. Maybe she was trying to warn you, or maybe she was trying to scare you into dropping out of the game show," Margaret said. "It would increase her odds of winning."

Ruth stiffened her back. "If that was her plan, it was a big mistake. Ruth Carpenter is not a quitter."

Gloria wandered over to the dining room window and stared out at the large tree. "Do you still have the wig you dug out of the dumpster yesterday?"

"I do."

"Perfect. I think Ivy Barnett is one of the keys to this mystery. Ruth, you need to contact Ivy, tell her you know she's the one who called the post office, that you're also certain you know who killed Amy Mahoney and you need her help."

"I do?" Ruth asked.

"Yes, you do," Gloria nodded.

Chapter 18

Ruth frowned at the small recording device. "You know how I hate these things, Gloria. I like to be the recorder, not the recordee."

"You'll be a little of both," Gloria said. "Remember, all you gotta do is convince Ivy that Travis Baexter plans to take her out, too. Drop it on her as a bombshell first, try to catch her off balance."

"Okay. You're packing heat?" Ruth asked.

"Yes, and so is Lucy." Gloria pointed to Lucy's jeep, parked on the other side of the playground.

"Margaret has the entrance and exit covered. If Ivy tries to pull anything funny, Margaret can chase her down."

Ruth shifted her gaze confirming the location of Margaret and her red Tesla. "Why am I so nervous?"

"Because I'm almost certain this woman is somehow involved in Amy Mahoney's death," Gloria said. "I'm not sure how, and that's the missing piece of the puzzle. Bluff her out. I think she'll sing like a canary."

"I see her over there, getting out of a silver SUV."

"Go get her!" Gloria said.

Ruth exited Gloria's car and headed to the park and a nearby bench.

Ivy Barnett spotted Ruth and slowly made her way over. "Hello Ruth."

"Hello Ivy. Thanks for meeting me."

"You're welcome." Ivy shifted uneasily. "You said you had some information about Amy Mahoney's death. I'm trying to figure out why you called me instead of going directly to the police."

"Because I'm almost certain you called the post office the other day and left me a message, warning me that someone was trying to frame me. You know who killed Amy Mahoney." Ruth hurried on. "I think you and Travis Baexter concocted a plan to take Amy Mahoney out of the competition. Amy somehow suspected Baexter was after her, but for some reason, believed I was in cahoots with him, too, which is why she attacked me after the first round of elimination the other day."

Ivy's face grew pale. "I...don't know what you're talking about," she sputtered.

"I wasn't supposed to make it to the final round of competition and neither was Amy Mahoney. It was supposed to be you and Travis Baexter. When Travis didn't make the cut, he moved on to Plan B, which you may or may not have known about...to sneak into the maze and take either

Amy Mahoney or me out. Amy was the unlucky one."

"That's ridiculous." Ivy turned to go.

"Is it? You know a lot about the game show rules. I decided that maybe I needed to know a bit more about the rules myself. It's interesting that if one or more of the contestants are eliminated during or after the final round, the next player, possibly two, move up in position."

She continued. "If Mahoney died and I was disqualified, then Travis would've made the cut. He would've automatically been added to the list of contestants...exactly how the plan was originally supposed to work."

"You have no proof. I had nothing to do with Amy's death. Travis hasn't confessed. It's your word against his, and there's more evidence pointing to you than to Travis."

"I have a wig in a safe spot that might prove otherwise. My theory is Travis lost in the first round, so he snuck into the back of the convention hall. My guess is he stashed a syringe full of morphine, planning to take out Amy or me...or perhaps even both of us. After he finished his dirty deed, he snuck out the side panel, exited the back door and tossed the wig in the dumpster. A well thought out murder, except that I'm betting some of Travis' own hair is stuck inside the wig, the perfect spot for the investigators to find DNA."

Ivy lowered her eyes and Ruth went in for the kill. "I'm sure once the authorities start questioning Travis, he's gonna spill all and implicate you. That's why I'm here...to return the favor. Turn Travis in before he's picked up and questioned, and the judge might cut you a break. If you had nothing to do with Amy's death, the truth will come out."

Ivy's eyes darted around the park. "I didn't know Travis was going to kill Amy," she whispered. "He threatened me that if I talked, he was going to pin it all on me since I was in the maze when Amy died."

"Maybe you weren't aware of Travis' backup plan. If he double-crossed once, he'll do it again."

Ivy's face crumpled, the seriousness of the situation sinking in. "I'll never make it to the Guinness Book of World Records now."

Ruth shook her head. "That would be the least of my worries."

***

"Welcome to Dash for Cash ladies and gentlemen. My name is Bob Larker, your host. We've had quite an exciting week here in Grand Rapids, Michigan. But nothing compares to the excitement of being a contestant on Dash for Cash!"

"Let's bring down our contestants." Bob glanced at the list he was holding. "Desiree Warner, come on down. You're our first contestant on Dash for Cash."

A tall, athletic woman scrambled down the center staircase and jogged to the front of the stage, shaking hands with the game show host. "Desiree, a former Montbay County corrections officer, now works as a personal fitness trainer."

"Next in line is Lane Jorgensen. Lane, a computer programmer from Detroit, is a new father." A young, bookish man with cropped blond locks sauntered down the steps. When he reached the stage, he shook Bob Larker's hand and joined Desiree.

"All of the contestants are going to have to work hard to beat Brent Gorley. Brent is a video game designer, and has even created his own version of Dash for Cash."

"Who is that?" Dot whispered.

"He was the next contestant in line after Mahoney died and Travis was disqualified," Gloria said.

Brent made his way down the steps and shook Bob's hand before taking his place next to Lane.

"Some of you may recognize the name of our next contestant, Ivy Barnett. The other contestants are going to have their work cut out for them competing against Ivy, who is on track to join the prestigious Guinness Book of World Records for the number of times on a game show."

Ivy bounded down the steps and jogged across the stage to join the others, her face flushed and she was grinning from ear to ear.

"Ivy shouldn't get too complacent, because she's got some stiff competition. Our final contestant is Ruth Carpenter, all the way from the small town of Belhaven, Michigan. Ruth, come on down."

Lucy placed her fingers in her mouth and whistled loudly as a beaming Ruth descended the steps and joined the other contestants on stage.

Gloria cupped her hands to her mouth and began to hoot and holler, joined by Rose, Alice and the other Garden Girls.

She shook Bob's hand and took her place on the stage.

"I'm glad there was a happy ending," Andrea whispered.

"Me too," Gloria said. "Travis Baexter is in jail, right where he should be."

"Ivy was lucky the investigators cut her some slack," Margaret chimed in.

"There was no evidence linking Ivy to the murders, unlike Travis and the hairs in the wig," Gloria said. "I guess our dumpster diving paid off, after all. I have to believe Ivy had no idea Travis planned to kill off his competitors and frame the other contestants."

"I still can't comprehend how someone could take another person's life over a silly game show," Dot said.

"It wasn't just the game show," Gloria said. "From what Ruth heard, Baexter confessed that Amy Mahoney had been taunting him, that his father was on the brink of being fired from the show and her uncle was going to do the firing. I guess he figured he could kill two birds with one stone, revenge for his father and eliminate his competition."

"They're about to get started," Lucy interrupted.

The first round was a series of trivia questions, all related to living in Michigan. Lane Jorgensen missed the most and exited the stage. Brent Gorley was next.

They were down to the three women in the second round, this one an endurance competition on the dreadmill, the one that Ruth mentioned dreading the most. The goal was for each contestant to walk on a treadmill, all the while balancing a tennis ball on top of a tennis racket.

Gloria was certain the dreadmill would be Ruth's downfall, but she hung on until Desiree Warner lost her footing and fell off.

"Well folks," Bob Larker said. "This is the moment we've all been waiting for. We have our finalists...Ruth Carpenter and Ivy Barnett."

Gloria watched as two of the show's crewmembers wheeled a square Plexiglas box onto the stage. "Ladies and Gentlemen, we have one more competition." He pointed to a large floor-to-ceiling curtain. "The runner up will get to select a mystery gift behind curtain number one or..." Bob Larker took several steps back. "Curtain number two."

He turned to Ruth and Ivy. "Ladies, even the runner-up prizes are fabulous, but we all know what you're here for." He pointed to the box.

The crowd began to chant. "Dash for Cash! Dash for Cash!"

"You've got that right folks." He turned his attention to Ruth and Ivy. "The goal in this round is to dash around the cash cube, circle back behind our stage area, and maneuver through the obstacle course with the final goal to be the first

266

contestant to reach the big red button over there. The first person to press the big red button will enter the cash grab booth for a chance to win..." Bob Larker paused dramatically. "Up to a hundred thousand dollars!"

The crowd cheered wildly and Ruth began to rub her hands together.

"It's time to get this game started." Bob led Ivy and Ruth to a strip of bright yellow tape.

"Are you nervous?" Bob stuck the microphone in Ivy's face.

"Not at all Bob," Ivy smiled warmly. "Although I have to say that Ruth will undoubtedly give me a run for my money...literally."

The crowd chuckled.

Bob stepped close to Ruth. "Ruth, are you ready to take down Ivy, a game show champion?"

"If I can," Ruth said honestly. "All I can say is let the best woman win."

"Okay folks." Bob stepped out of the way. "Ladies, it's a go on the buzzer."

Gloria held her breath and waited for the buzzer. Her stomach twisted in a knot and she wondered if she was more nervous than Ruth. "Go Ruth go!"

Lucy reached for Gloria's hand and squeezed. Gloria grabbed Margaret's hand. The women all joined hands, squeezing tightly as the buzzer sounded.

Gloria kept her eyes trained on Ruth the entire time. It was a dead heat from the beginning, all the way around the stage, until Ruth and Ivy reached the obstacle course. Ruth was a nose length ahead until her tennis shoe caught on a tire rim and she lost her momentum.

Taking advantage of Ruth's stumble, Ivy pounded her way through the remaining tires and raced to the big red button, flinging her body against it.

Ding, ding. Ivy began to hop up and down, clapping her hands as the crowd cheered.

Gloria and the others clapped politely and watched as Ruth made her way to the winner where she gave her competitor a victorious high five.

"Well, Ruth." Bob placed a light hand across Ruth's shoulders. "The odds were stacked against you since Ivy is a pro." He shook his head. "I have to say, if you hadn't caught the tip of your shoe on the tire, you might have beaten her."

Ruth said the first thing that popped into her head. "I'm going to toss these in the trash as soon as I get home. Traitors."

Bob chuckled. "It isn't all bad." He turned so that Ruth and he faced the two curtains. "You're going to walk away with a very nice consolation prize. The choice is yours...would you like the mystery prize behind curtain number one or curtain number two?"

"I would like to make an educated guess. Why don't you tell me what's behind them?" Ruth joked.

Bob patted Ruth's shoulder. "You know I can't do that."

"If you don't mind, I would like to consult my friends." Ruth turned to face the crowd, her eyes searching the audience until she found the Garden Girls. "There they are." She pointed to the women and they all waved.

Bob waved. "So, Ruth, which curtain are you going to choose?"

Gloria held up two fingers. Margaret held up one. It was a pretty even split on the number each of them thought Ruth should choose. "I'm gonna have to go with curtain number...two."

"Curtain number two." Bob and Ruth shifted until they faced the curtain again. "Okay Marianna, let's show Ruth what's behind curtain number two."

The elegantly attired female hostess glided across the stage, grasped the edge of the curtain and walked it back, revealing a shiny new speedboat.

A second announcer began to speak. "Congratulations Ruth Carpenter. You've won a brand new Sea Ray SLX-W 230. The SLX-W offers refined luxury and a powerful wave." The announcer droned on about the newly revamped Sea Ray, which boasted a high-tech screen, giving the driver full control over the surf settings and the shape of the wave. "Bob, this is a fine piece of machinery, perfect for any boater in the family. The ship's deep hull smooths the ride even on the choppiest of waters."

"What is Ruth going to do with a fancy fishing boat?" Lucy whispered.

"Loan it to Paul," Gloria grinned. "Poor Ruth. I wonder what was behind the other curtain."

"I bet she does, too," Margaret said.

Ruth thanked Bob, stepped off the stage and disappeared from sight.

Bob joined Ivy and they made their way to the cash booth. "Congratulations, Ivy. You're one tough cookie to beat."

"Ruth was pretty tough herself," Ivy admitted.

"She sure was," Bob said. "I'm going to guess you've studied the cash booth, but let me repeat the rules. You must remain in an upright position. You can't bend down. You'll be disqualified if you pick bills off the floor or trap them against the sides of the box. You have thirty seconds to grab as much cash as possible and stuff it in the box. Are you ready?"

Ivy sucked in a breath and nodded. "Yes."

A second stagehand opened the door and Ivy stepped inside. The whir of the blower filled the stage, and the timer began as money began to blast into the air. Ivy frantically grabbed the bills and stuffed them into the box. When the timer chimed, the blower stopped and the remaining cash fluttered to the floor.

Ivy stepped out of the box and the stagehand pulled the box, filled with bills off the side while the audience applauded.

"Congratulations Ivy. It looks as if you made quite a haul."

"Thank you Bob." Bob accompanied Ivy off the stage and wrapped up the show.

Gloria and her friends waited for what seemed like forever for Ruth to join them. Finally, Ruth emerged waving a set of keys. "Well, I got a nice boat out of it."

"Congratulations Ruth." Gloria patted her back. "Paul will be thrilled."

"If you're not gonna use it, sell it and take the cash," Lucy suggested.

"You'll have to pay taxes on the cash value," Margaret pointed out.

"Great." Ruth frowned. "I asked the contest supervisor if he could give me a rough estimate of the value of the boat and he said it lists for right around $65k."

"Wow." Rose's eyes grew wide. "That's a chunk of change."

"You betcha," Ruth smiled. "I'm not one to gloat, but Ivy only managed to grab $45k in cash, so I guess it makes me the big winner after all."

"You can take us all down to Dot's for dinner," Lucy said.

"Yes, and now we can put this Dash for Cash contest in the history books," Margaret added.

"Maybe," Ruth said. "While we were waiting to sign some paperwork, Ivy told me about another new contest coming to town. It's called Mystery Puzzle Play. It's a team competition and we could all team up and play together."

"No!" Margaret, Lucy, Andrea, Dot, Rose, Alice, Eleanor and Gloria said in unison.

274

"We have more than enough excitement in Belhaven without competing in game shows," Gloria said.

"Amen to that." Rose agreed. "Speaking of excitement, I've been working on a new potion."

"I rest my case," Gloria said. "Now...who's ready to go home?"

The end.

If you enjoyed reading "Dash For Cash," please take a moment to leave a review. It would be greatly appreciated. Thank you.

The series continues...Book 19 in the "Garden Girls Cozy Mystery" series coming soon!

Books in This Series

Who Murdered Mr. Malone? Book 1
Grandkids Gone Wild: Book 2
Smoky Mountain Mystery: Book 3
Death by Dumplings: Book 4
Eye Spy: Book 5
Magnolia Mansion Mysteries: Book 6
Missing Milt: Book 7
Bully in the 'Burbs: Book 8
Fall Girl: Book 9
Home for the Holidays: Book 10
Sun, Sand, and Suspects: Book 11
Look Into My Ice: Book 12
Forget Me Knot: Book 13
Nightmare in Nantucket: Book 14
Greed with Envy: Book 15
Dying for Dollars: Book 16
Stranger Among Us: Book 17
Dash For Cash: Book 18
Book 19: Coming Soon!
Garden Girls Box Set I – (Books 1-3)
Garden Girls Box Set II – (Books 4-6)
Garden Girls Box Set III – (Books 7-9)

Save 50-90% on Your Next Cozy Mystery

Get the Best Prices on Hope Callaghan Books

Meet the Author

Hope loves to connect with her readers! Connect with her today!

Visit **hopecallaghan.com/newsletter** for special offers, free books, and soon-to-be-released books!

Email: hope@hopecallaghan.com

Facebook: www.facebook.com/authorhopecallaghan/

Hope Callaghan is an author who loves to write Christian books, especially Christian Mystery and Cozy Mystery books. She has written more than 50 mystery books (and counting) in five series.

In March 2017, Hope won a Mom's Choice Award for her book, "Key to Savannah," Book 1 in the Made in Savannah Cozy Mystery Series.

Born and raised in a small town in West Michigan, she now lives in Florida with her husband.

She is the proud mother of one daughter and a stepdaughter and stepson. When she's not doing the thing she loves best - writing books - she enjoys cooking, traveling and reading books.

Zesty Slow Cooker Chicken Barbecue Recipe

Ingredients:

6 - skinless, boneless chicken breasts
1 - 28 oz. bottle of barbecue sauce (We used Sweet Baby Ray's Original Sauce)
½ cup Italian salad dressing (We used Ken's Steak House Lite Northern Italian Dressing & Marinade)
2 – medium cloves of garlic, chopped
2 – medium yellow onions, chopped

Directions:

- Place chopped onion and garlic in bottom of crockpot.
- Place thawed chicken breasts on top of onion and garlic.
- Add small amount of water so that the garlic doesn't burn.
- Cook on high for three hours or until meat reaches internal temperature of 165 degrees F.
- Remove chicken, allow to cool for handling.
- Shred chicken and put back in crockpot.
- Mix barbecue sauce and Italian dressing thoroughly.
- Pour mixture over shredded chicken and mix thoroughly.
- Cover chicken and cook for another hour.

Ruth's Creamy Chicken and Wild Rice Soup Recipe

Ingredients:

1 cup celery, chopped
2 medium cloves of garlic, chopped
2 small yellow onions, chopped
5 cups chicken broth
2 cups water
3 cooked, boneless chicken breasts, shredded
1 - 4.5 package quick cooking long grain and wild rice with seasoning packet (we used Rice-A-Roni brand)
½ tsp. salt
½ tsp. black pepper
¾ cup all-purpose flour
½ cup butter
2 cups heavy cream (we substituted with 2% milk)

Directions:
- In large pot, melt butter. Add onion and celery. Sauté until the onion is clear.
- Add garlic and sauté lightly.
- Add flour, seasoning packet, salt and pepper. Mix thoroughly to make a roux.
- Add broth, water, and chicken. Stir.
- Bring just to boiling, and then stir in rice.
- Cover and turn down heat to simmer for 10 minutes.

- Add milk. Stir. Cook over medium heat for another 10 minutes, stirring often.
- Remove cover and remove from heat.
- Let sit for 10 minutes to thicken.

Made in the USA
Monee, IL
15 September 2022